THE CROW™

city of angels

THE CROW™

city of angels

A novel by Chet Williamson
Based on the screenplay by David S. Goyer
Based on characters created by James O'Barr

BOULEVARD BOOKS, NEW YORK

THE CROW: CITY OF ANGELS

A Boulevard Book / published by arrangement with
ERPEC Releasing, Inc.

PRINTING HISTORY
Boulevard edition / August 1996

The Putnam Berkley World Wide Web site address is
http://www.berkley.com

ISBN:1-57297-218-1

BOULEVARD
Boulevard Books are published by The Berkley Publishing Group,
200 Madison Avenue, New York, New York 10016.
BOULEVARD and its logo are trademarks
belonging to Berkley Publishing Corporation.

PRINTED IN THE UNITED STATES OF AMERICA

10 9 8 7 6 5 4 3 2 1

THE CITY IS OF NIGHT; PERCHANCE OF DEATH,
BUT CERTAINLY OF NIGHT. . . .
—James Thomson,
"The City of Dreadful Night"

From Sarah's journal:

*I believe there's a place where the restless souls
wander. Burdened by the weight of their own sadness, they cannot enter heaven.*

*And so they wait, trapped between our world
and the next, endlessly searching for a way to rid
themselves of their pain—in the hopes that somehow, someday, they will be reunited with the ones
they love.*

I believe it's true, for I have seen it happen. . . .

There is a land. . . .

There is a land the living cannot know. It is a land
where the mist hangs in the air like an infinite number

1

of tears, coalescing into a thick cloud of pain and sorrow that seems as impenetrable as it is endless.

There is nothing else. No hills or valleys define the barren landscape. No trees mar its sodden surface. Nothing grows there but grief.

Through that primordial realm of shadow a bird flies. It is a crow, its feathers black as night, so black that it seems to draw all the light around it into the soft sheen of its feathers, and it glimmers with that stolen light. Its eyes are a golden brown, the color of newly dead leaves, the shade of regret, of hopes lost and dreams shattered. Its beak and claws glint like black steel, cold and deadly.

Something else moves in this loveless land. It bears the shape of a warrior mounted on a horse. The steed gallops through the blinding mist, as though it knows there is nothing but the hanging tears to halt its swift progress. It makes no sound as it runs. No foam drips from its mouth, and its chest does not move, nor do its nostrils flare. It seems to have unending strength. Its legs, a black blur in the mist, are tireless machines, driving it onward with its rider.

That rider's baleful eyes shine behind a face that seems to be a mask. It is of the whiteness of chalk covering yellow bone. Black accents highlight it, outlining the grim mouth, turning the corners of the lips upward, creating a false smile in a land where smiles are unknown.

The blackness also surrounds the eyes. A broader scar of black extends from the brows to the cheeks, a dark slash miraculously sparing the eyes themselves. It

2

is as though an ebony tear drops from the center of each eye, and rises from them as well.

It is a mask of laughter and of despair, a face of pained and bitter irony.

The horse and rider plunge through the mist, never seeming to reach their destination, if indeed they have one. And above them the crow drifts, its feathers heavy with bright darkness, with black light, with grief. . . .

With hope.

Curve saw the crow settle down on the shipping container. Ugly freakin' bird, and only about twenty yards away. He would have pulled out his piece and blown it into a cloud of feathers and blood if his hands hadn't been otherwise occupied.

He looked down and grinned at the crude stamp on the glassine envelope that he now ripped open. "'Lo, you little prick," he mumbled to the cartoon imp who looked up at him with a shit-eating grin and a cheery thumbs-up. *That's right, kiddies,* it seemed to say. *We're havin' some fun now.* . . .

Trinity. Best drug in Curve's pissed and addled memory. The Father, Son, and Holy Shit and a great big brain-bomb all rolled into one. Took the top of your head clean off and let the angels fly in, take a cosmic crap, and roar on out again.

Curve breathed in long and hard through his congested nose. He wanted to get his sinuses as clear as possible so that Trinity could rush in unimpeded and send his mind to that bright nirvana that the combination of the drug and his already whacked-out brain created.

3

The night and the docks didn't help to clear his nose. He breathed in a nice unhealthy dose of poison along with the air. The spot where the river met the sea was filled with as much shit and garbage as water anymore. The whole damn City of Angels was polluted with chemicals and by-products and crap he couldn't pronounce. And it was polluted with him too.

Yeah, Curve was part of the pollution, not the solution, and proud of it. He made sure he was sitting firmly on the seat of his chopper so that the rush wouldn't knock him down. Then he ducked his head, jammed his nose right into the glassine, and sucked in like an industrial vac, turning the envelope inside out with the strength of his snort.

Badda-*bing,* badda-*bang,* badda-*CHOW*!

Oh yeah, the bells rang and the sirens wailed and Trinity peeled open his skull like a stripper rolling down her panties. Then Trinity screwed his brain and it came twenty or thirty times until the angels were done with him and flew away.

But the crow hadn't. It was still sitting there, a big ugly bird on a big ugly dock in the biggest, ugliest, and baddest city in the world, and the black son-of-a-bitch was looking at something, and when Curve looked where the crow was looking, he remembered why he was down on this shithole dock in the first place.

Light flared into his eyes, and at first he thought the dark angels were coming back, but then he realized it was just the light of Nemo's camcorder. He ran a hand over the top of his head to make sure that his skull really wasn't open to the elements. The feel of his long blond hair against his palm reassured him, and he lit a

4

cigarette. Tobacco tasted better when he was high on Trinity. Hell, *everything* was better on Trinity.

He got off his bike and admired again the custom painting on his pearl-drop gas tank. A woman with the biggest tits imaginable was doing the wild thing with the Grim Reaper, Death himself, and loving it. *Death screws us all in the end,* Curve thought. *We might as well get to know the old bastard first.*

He looked back at the end of the pier just a few yards away. Nemo was getting off on this all right, dancing around the guy and his kid with the camera, getting every last twitch of their faces, every single bit of fear captured on videotape. The old sleaze-hound loved to look. Curve always thought if you gave Nemo the choice between boning and *watching*, Nemo would just watch and whack. When he wasn't working for Judah, he spent nearly all his time shoving tokens in the sticky slots at the Peep-O-Rama. He'd probably go home tonight and flick his chicken to the tape he was shooting now.

"Camera!" Nemo yelled as he moved around the father and son. The man was in his late twenties, and the boy was maybe eight or so. Curve couldn't guess kids' ages for shit. He had tried to forget his own childhood. It had sucked big time, a nightmare of beatings and burnings and things far worse.

What was so sacred about childhood? It was no different and just as cruel as adult life. As far as Curve was concerned, being a kid didn't save you. Kids were nothing special. Hell, everybody in the City of Angels, except for Judah's people, were victims, and kids were

5

just shorter victims, that was all. The good thing about them was that they died easier than adults.

"Action!" Nemo yelled, his long hair flying as he danced around the pair. "Action action *action*!"

"What ya want 'em to do, start dancin'?" Spider Monkey said dryly. He had a helluva point. The man and his kid were at the end of the pier. Daddy's right arm was linked with Sonny's left one, and their hands were tied behind their backs. They were kneeling side by side on the rough, weather-beaten boards. They weren't dancing, they weren't running. They weren't doing a damn thing but dying.

And crying. At least the kid was. "I'm sorry, Dad," Curve heard him blubber. "I'm sorry. . . . I didn't mean to look. . . ."

"It's okay, Danny," the father said. "It's okay." But it wasn't okay. It wasn't okay at all, and Big Daddy knew it, no matter how much he tried to reassure little Danny.

Danny. Typical little-kid name, for all the good it would do him. Little Danny didn't score any cute points with Kali, that was for sure. The bitch's eyes were as cold as the metal that made up sixty percent of her wardrobe. Heavy metal, heavy heart, that was Kali. She just stood there, watching the little family's fear, feeding on it, waiting for the best part. She wasn't smiling, but she was getting off on it for sure.

Curve saw her eyes blaze with pleasure when Nemo slapped the father hard across the face. "Makeup!" he yelled, and hit him again. "Get some color in those cheeks for the close-ups!" Nemo grinned, showing blackened teeth. Christ, Curve thought, with all the

6

money Nemo got from Judah, you'd think he could have those rotten teeth fixed. Maybe *that* was why he never got any real pussy.

Nemo slapped the boy's face then, not as hard as he had struck the father, but hard enough to rock the kid's head back. "Stop it!" the father shouted. "You son-of-a-bitch, leave him alone!"

Old Pops had a lot of balls. He was in no position to be making demands. What was his name anyway? Curve thought for a moment, and the name came through the buzz-fuzz that Trinity had laid on his brain.

Corven. Ashe Corven. Goofy goddam name. But then, he thought, maybe no goofier than Curve and Kali and Spider Monkey. Of course, those were names they had chosen, not been given by some artsy-fartsy mama. Ashe. Yeah, Ashe was an ashehole who was going to become ashes to ashes.

"Did you tell me somethin', man?" Nemo asked Ashe Corven, and then hit the kid again, this time harder, backhanding him. "I said *makeup*!" Nemo yelled so loudly that flecks of spittle glistened on Corven's face.

The boy started to pray in a language Curve didn't understand. He thought it was Latin.

"Learn that in Catholic school, little guy?" Spider Monkey said, crouching next to the tied-up pair and holding a large marigold in front of the kid's face as though inviting him to smell it. His lean and gangly frame made him look easy to break, but Spider Monkey was all tough and stringy muscle. "You're wasting your time, *angelito*. Nobody's up there listening."

7

"Maybe he oughta pray to Saint Lucas!" Nemo said, still gazing into the eyepiece of the camcorder, whirling around to capture everything.

"Shut up, man," Spider Monkey told him. "You don't know shit. It's *San* Lucas—la Noche de *San* Lucas."

Spider Monkey was right. October 29. La Noche de San Lucas. Curve didn't know what the hell it was for—just a couple of nights before the Day of the Dead, as far as he was concerned. But then that was nothing special either. Every day was the day of the dead when you worked for Judah Earl.

Still, Spider Monkey seemed to take this religious shit half seriously sometimes, and now he held his marigold out in front of Ashe Corven's face. The sudden burst of yellow orange seemed to brighten the mud-brown dock. "Flowers for the dead, señor?" Spider Monkey asked almost gently.

Corven only stared at him. There was a lot of hate in the man's eyes. He was either brave or stupid. Or maybe he was just realistic. He knew what was coming, and didn't see any reason to kiss ass at this point.

"No?" said Spider Monkey. He stuck a look of mock sorrow on his long face. "Suit yourself, then." Spider Monkey looked at the flower, then tucked it behind his right ear and stood up.

Curve sniffed once more, fisted the remains of the white powder from his nose, and rubbed his knuckle on his gums. It was time. Everybody had had their fun. He walked up to Kali. "Let's get this over with," he said. "Judah's waiting."

Kali slowly took out her revolver and began to load

8

it. This was foreplay for Kali. She inserted each bullet as methodically and carefully as if they were live grenades. Bitch. She was taking her own sweet time just to spit in Curve's eye, and he didn't like it a bit. But he was damned if he was going to give her the satisfaction of showing her he was pissed. He kept his face as flat and expressionless as hers, and waited.

It seemed like hours, but it might just have been the Trinity playing with his time sense. At last she flicked her wrist, and he heard the sharp snap of the cylinder locking into place. Kali slowly walked over to Ashe Corven and his kid, moving as sensuously and as menacingly as the goddess of death whose name she had stolen.

The kid, Danny, had stopped praying. His eyes didn't move from Kali's serpentine approach. "I'm scared, Dad," he said in a whisper.

"I know," Ashe Corven said. Curve thought he was trying to sound brave. But Corven's voice cracked, and his face softened, and Curve saw fear there; not for himself, but for his son. Curve knew what would happen now. It was pleading time.

"Listen to me," Corven said. "*Please!* He's just a kid. Let him go, he can't hurt you! He doesn't even know who you are. Kill me, but please don't—"

Hurt my son? Yeah, Curve thought. That's probably what he would have said next, if Kali hadn't brought up her revolver and plowed a bullet right through little Danny's thin chest.

CROW: A LARGE BLACK BIRD THAT FEEDS UPON
THE CARCASSES OF BEASTS.

—Johnson's *Dictionary*

"NOOOOO!"

It came from deep inside him, from a hitherto unknown land on the map of his soul. He screamed as his
heart tightened, clenching like a thick red fist. He had
not imagined this. He had admitted the possibility, but
had not even conceived of the power it would wield
over him.

He knew that he would die, that they would probably both die for what they had seen. But all the imagining, all the fears, all the deaths died before death
itself had not prepared him for this, for the brightest
light of his life to be snuffed out. He did not expect so
deep a blackness, so deep an abyss. He had not known
that one could fall forever into total darkness, and he
knew that this was to be his fate.

11

When Danny fell backward, Ashe had fallen with him, twisting so that his son's bloody chest was against his own, and Danny's eyes were inches away from his. He saw the life flee from them, and he could not reach out a hand to bring it back, could not draw death to him instead, for death was greedy. It wanted them both.

Something, a glint of orange light, whizzed over Ashe's head, and for a mad moment he thought that it might be Danny's soul soaring away. But the angry hiss told him that it was only a cigarette butt, flicked away by the one called Curve, striking the foul waters where the river met the sea. The Styx. River of the dead. Dead.

Dead.

"Nothing personal, sport," he heard Curve's gravel voice say. "Guess you were just in the wrong place at the wrong time."

Then the shots came. He heard them distinctly, three of them. He felt them too, all three, enter his back. He felt his skin burst, his bones shatter, his heart and lungs tear apart, spilling blood and air into him, out of him, felt his head fill with pressure as the blood rushed into his ears, into his brain, drowning him. The pain did not stop. It went on and on, both the pain of death and the greater pain of loss.

From somewhere high above, far below, he heard a voice, and at first he thought it might be God, but he knew he was wrong when the words found meaning in his brain:

Drop 'em. Let's get this cluster fuck on the road.

He felt what was left to feel in his body being pressed close to Danny's. For a moment there was a sensation of curving, turning, rolling, and then the voice again:

Bon voyage, shitheads . . .

He fell. He seemed to fall forever, and his open eyes saw the dead face of his beloved son (*in whom I am well pleased*), past him the black, poisoned sky, something darker against it, and forms, shapes with heads and shoulder, the ones who did this, who killed him.

Who killed Danny.

Then he entered the water, not with a splash, but with the embrace of soft, cold arms, pulling gently down. The light faded, and looking up past dear dead Danny at the world was like looking through cloudy glass that slowly got thicker and thicker until it banished all the light. Ashe's only movement now was in sympathy to the eddies of the vile waters. He could still hear, like a faraway drum, the sound of his own heart beating, struggling to close its new openings with blood, trying to save itself by pouring away Ashe's life.

In the stygian darkness, as the beating grew slower and finally ceased altogether, Ashe somehow saw his blood, his life drifting up and away from him, spreading over him like a cloud, a blanket, like the wings of an angel . . .

. . . or the wings of a great bird.

The Crow floated upward through the murky waters, riding on the currents, rising as gently as Ashe and his son sank, until at last it burst from beneath the black surface, soaring into the air with one strong cry of triumph, the water falling away from it like a cast-off skin, like sins renounced.

From filthy water into filthy air it flew, high over the city, past ragged strands of smog hovering like an army of sickly ghosts. The Crow rode the thermals above the City of Angels, an urban sprawl riven in one place by fire, in another by flood, in still another by earthquake. The lights below, so bright and boastful on the ground, looked pale and ineffectual to the Crow's gold-brown eyes.

The Crow flew over a bridge that spanned the Styx. It was a river made by man, created proudly and quickly by the greed of those who ruled the City of Angels. That same greed had defiled it even more efficiently and ruthlessly.

Past the bridge, the bird descended. It swept down through caverns whose surfaces were concrete and glass, soiled with pigeon droppings and industrial grime. The shifting searchlights of police helicopters darted across the man-made canyons, always searching, seldom finding.

But the Crow's eyes saw everything: the hulks of cars littering the streets like insect husks, the homeless who sheltered inside and under them. It saw the wicked and the weary, those who walked in fear and were preyed upon, and the predators, cruel ones whose souls had been smothered years before. It saw those who were sleepless from pain or despair, and those who slept in spite of their pain.

It saw Sarah.

From Sarah's journal:

They say that time cancels pain. I don't know about that. Eight years ago I lost two of my best friends. Two thousand miles later I find I'm still living in the past.

Every night when I close my eyes the dreams come. That's how the dead talk to us, I guess. In the dark, when our souls are off wandering.

I just wish I understood what they were telling me.

Sarah was in the middle of a dream when the Crow landed on the sill of her open window and looked into her loft. Its small but piercing eyes saw an attractive woman lying in a rumpled bed. Though she was in her early twenties, there were far more years of living etched into her troubled face. She had survived struggles in her life, and though she had won, the battles had taken their toll.

Now, in her dream, she fought another battle, the battle to understand what she saw but could not hear. She saw Eric and Shelly again, her friends of long ago, when she was a child and needed friends desperately. They looked as they had when she had seen them last, on Devil's Night when she was still a kid, right before Top Dollar's gang had killed them both.

In the dream, Eric and Shelly were happy again, at rest and together in some wonderful place that Sarah could only get a brief glimpse of. But although she could tell that they were content with each other in some land beyond life and death, she also knew that they were trying to tell her something. They spoke, but she couldn't hear their words, and when they gestured, it looked to Sarah as though they were underwater.

You're always underwater in a dream, she thought, and tried to move closer to them. But it was like walking in jelly, and she could not move, but could only stand there impotently, knowing that what they were trying to tell her was important, and feeling more stupid than she had ever felt before, because she could not understand them.

Then Eric seemed to gaze at something behind her, and he suddenly pointed, as though if she only looked at where he intended, she would solve the riddle. She swung around in the dream, and she was in the dream no longer.

She opened her eyes in her own loft, and before she could clear the sleep from them, something moved at her window, rising and vanishing into the night. She thought she heard the rustling sound of wings, but saw only darkness against the night.

The Crow, she thought.

Dreaming of Eric, and then seeing the Crow. It was too great a coincidence. The Crow had to be what Eric was pointing at, didn't it?

Or was the Crow ever there at all? she wondered. Had she dreamed it too?

The Crow had started it all eight years before. It had allowed Eric to come back to life, brought him up from the grave, alive again, but nearly invincible. There had been a score to settle with Top Dollar's men, and Eric had settled it. With blood and violence he had assuaged his pain and Shelly's, and returned to death again.

16

Sarah knew that it was not revenge. It was justice, justice that could not be imposed by the living. But until it was imposed, until the guilty were punished, Eric could never be reunited with Shelly.

But they were reunited, and Top Dollar and all his gang were dead and in their graves for years. So what was Eric trying to say?

And why had the Crow come back?

Gabriel leaped onto the foot of the bed, startling Sarah from her thoughts. "Oh, Gabriel," Sarah said, and hugged the cat, so that it started to purr. Gabriel was part of her memories too. He had belonged to Eric and Shelly, and Sarah had adopted him after their deaths. No matter where she went or what she went through, Gabriel had stayed by her side, fending for himself when she was in no position to feed or care for him.

But she was together now, and determined to stay that way. Her life wasn't perfect, but she was happy with it. She had her own place, her own business, and a few friends.

Sarah looked around her loft contentedly. It was filled with treasures, most of which she had found in various thrift shops. The furniture, though threadbare, was comfortable, and the entire loft had a warm and earthy ambience in sharp contrast to the squalor on the other side of the walls.

Still, she was alone. Beneath her were only two floors of empty storerooms, and below that a warehouse. No neighbors, no attachments, and no passions. But it was enough for now.

She padded barefoot to the arching half-circle window and looked out upon the jungle below. As she gazed down at the hunters and the hunted, she felt like the lord of a peaceful island in a stormy and frenzied sea. The place was hers, and she could do whatever she liked in it.

What she liked to do most was paint, and the canvases, both finished and those in progress that leaned against the walls or sat on a half-dozen battered easels, were proof of her inclination. Most were symbolist works, turbulent and brooding. All were deeply emotional, and many viewers would have found them upsetting. She paused before the painting she was presently working on, and examined it closely.

It showed a woman who resembled Sarah being cradled in the arms of a man with a pale face and sorrowful features. All around the central figures were dozens of other figures, seen as if through a mist. Their faces were nearly blank, but her skillful brushes had given them looks of slight concern and pity, as though they yearned to aid the lovers in the foreground, but had lost all ability to do so. It was the only way that Sarah knew to illustrate a legion of the watchful dead.

She looked away from the work, shook herself as though to cast off a nightmare, and headed toward the bathroom. There she stripped off her nightshirt, revealing a pair of black angel wings sweeping over her shoulder blades. The graceful tattoo work extended across her back and down both upper arms, ending in delicately detailed primary feathers just above her elbows. Her slim body was further ornamented by two rings, one in her right nipple, the other in her navel.

Sarah stepped into the shower and closed the curtain

18

behind her. Then she turned on the water and shut her eyes, anticipating the spray. The water struck her face, piercing and cold . . .

. . . and she saw, for only a moment, another face, a man's face, pale and horrified, sinking into dark and muddy waters. . . .

Her eyes snapped open. The hard spray stung them, and she turned her head away, putting out a hand to the tile wall to steady herself and recover from the force of her vision.

When she was able to stop shaking, she gave herself a quick wash, then toweled off and got dressed. "Who was *that*?" she asked herself and Gabriel several times, but neither had an answer. "Who the hell was *that*?" She knew she had never seen the man before, so why had he pushed his way into her thoughts?

More than her thoughts—her very soul. She had seen him, but for that split second she had also felt his pain, his panic, his . . . grief.

Yes, there had been grief there, terrible psychic pain even worse than the physical pain that had momentarily coursed through her body. But where had he come from, and why had he come to her?

She sat down at her vanity table to try to pick some jewelry to wear. Maybe it would get this stranger and Eric and the Crow and *everything* off her mind for a minute. She chose a necklace that she often wore, a silver chain with a silver ankh, the symbol of eternity.

But the thought of eternity made her think of Eric and Shelly, and she looked at the mask she had hung on the wall by the vanity. It was made of white ceramic with a black-painted upturned smile and black accents above and below the vacant eyes. Shelly had kept it by her mirror in the loft she shared with Eric, and it was the face that Eric had painted on his own dead-alive flesh when he went searching for justice.

Sarah sighed and picked up the tarnished engagement ring that Shelly had worn. She held it so that the word inscribed on the inside caught the light:

Forever

Sarah had wanted to pick jewelry to forget, but now she remembered more clearly than ever. So many memories, so many ghosts.

Gabriel seemed to sense her mood, and rubbed against her legs. He meowed once, and in the forlorn sound Sarah heard a very human note of sadness. She picked up the cat, hugged him, and whispered, "Me too . . ."

Sarah had not worn Shelly's ring for a long time. The streets of the City of Angels were mean, and she had not wanted to take a chance on its being stolen. But now her need to feel closer to Shelly and Eric and whatever they were trying to tell her was stronger than her caution.

She threaded the ring onto her silver chain so that it fell next to the ankh. Then she slipped the necklace over her head, pulled on a jacket, and after giving Gabriel a final caress, headed out to the street. It was the middle of the night, but she couldn't sleep, and she wasn't afraid.

She knew how the night worked in the City of Angels.

At least there was no one sleeping in the entryway to her building when she left. The owner must have fixed the lock. She'd give it a week before it was busted again, and the vagrants were snoozing in the corners. Sarah really didn't care. Most of the homeless weren't violent. They just wanted a warm place to sleep for the night where the dogs wouldn't pee on them and the gangs wouldn't burn them. Poor bastards.

But she drew the compassion line at the door of her loft. It was as sound as a bank vault. She had spent nearly three hundred dollars on locks and bars, and her locksmith told her that a burglar would have needed high-yield plastique to breach her fortress.

Now she stepped out into the night and breathed in its ripeness. It was the smell of the city, a symphony of stenches composed of Oriental food, bus exhaust, industrial waste, old grease, and piss, but it was the only place she knew, the only air she smelled, and she was used to it. There were times she even liked it.

Sarah walked down the steps of her building, shutting her eyes as the wind kicked up bits of trash and grit. Among the flying debris were dozens of empty glassine envelopes with the familiar stamp of the grinning imp. "Friggin' Trinity," Sarah muttered as the dope leaves blew past.

It was the newest thing, the drug du jour, cheap enough for rat's ass junkies, but with a big enough payload for a well-heeled connoisseur. Sarah had never tried it. She had been clean for a long time, and planned to stay that way.

But those who had snorted the shit told her that it lasted longer than crack, was more calming than heroin, and zipped you up higher than speed. And if you wanted to see pretty colors and flowers, it gave

21

you a bigger polychrome blast than primo acid. In short, Trinity was your best friend, your dream drug. It did whatever the hell you wanted it to do. Trinity read your mind, and then fucked it.

The only downside was that addiction came fast and hard and certain. Once you had snorted up the joys of the imp, every other drug seemed like Pez, and real life seemed like an unflushed toilet in a cheap Mexican restaurant.

Slowly but surely the discarded, multicolored plastic crack vials, more numerous than cigarette butts, had vanished from the streets, replaced by the thrown-away glassine envelopes with the discarded smiling imp. What did the little bastard have to be so happy about? Sarah wondered. People used him up and threw him away, he was stepped on and run over, dissolved in the rain, and washed away into the sewers.

But he always came back. He was always there grinning at you from the sidewalk and the gutters. And every day there were more and more of him. Maybe that was why he was so damned happy. He could die and come back to life again, over and over.

Sarah slogged through the dust and the empty beer cans and the Trinity confetti, heading toward a coffee shop where she knew she could always get a decent cup of black stuff and some half-intelligent conversation at any time of the day or night. But her pace slowed, as though something were tugging on her foot. She lifted her Doc Martens, and saw that a wad of gum stuck to a Trinity sachet had wedged itself into her sole.

"Shit," she said, and untied the boot and pulled it

22

off. She was scraping the mess off on the edge of the curb and thinking bad thoughts about junkies who chewed gum, when she noticed the girl looking at her from a shadowed entryway that had long been missing its door.

The girl was about sixteen. Her face was pale, her hair dirty and stringy. She was hugging herself tightly and shaking like the Jell-O that Sarah's mother, Darla, had made on those rare occasions when she felt more like a mommy than a junkie whore. Sarah pegged the shakes as withdrawal, and the glassine envelopes at the girl's feet made her certain. As amazing as Trinity was, it didn't last forever, and it wasn't free.

Her boot was finally clean, and Sarah put it back on and walked toward the girl. She drew back, frightened and suspicious, clutching a purple bag with a beaded happy face sewn onto its cheap cloth. Sarah held her hands up in the age-old gesture of peace and looked at the entryway. In the semidarkness, she could make out big pieces of cardboard in a corner away from the stairs and a pile of rags scattered on top of them.

"Nice place you've got here," Sarah said. She hoped the girl wasn't beyond comprehending sarcasm.

She shivered again, and said something that Sarah didn't understand. "What?" Sarah asked.

"Noplace else to go," the girl whispered in a sand-paper voice.

Suddenly the girl seemed strangely familiar, and Sarah knew why. It was as though she were looking into a mirror a few years before. She was this girl, this lost soul trying to survive on the streets. Sarah had succeeded and come out of her hell, but not without help.

23

Maybe this was a way to pay back the ones who had cared about her.

"Got a name?" she asked the girl.

"Grace. So what?"

Sarah. So what? God, how she remembered all too well. How she wished she could forget. "So, Grace, how does some hot coffee sound? With real cream and real sugar." White powder that won't kill you, she thought. "Maybe a little food?"

The girl's eyes narrowed as she tried to tough it out, but she only shivered again, destroying the illusion of invincibility. "What do you want?" Of course she didn't trust her. She didn't trust anybody. Why should she? Look what the city had done to her.

Sarah tried to show her that she spoke true. "Nothing. I don't want a thing, Grace. I guess you just remind me of somebody I used to know."

The girl looked at her for a long time, like a wild dog that wanted a piece of meat, but feared to be touched by the person who offered it. At last she gave a reluctant nod.

As they walked out of the entryway, the girl shielded her eyes from the lights of the closed stores and the street lamps, and let Sarah lead her down the street toward the warmth of the coffee shop.

From a nearby rooftop, gold-brown eyes watched them go. The feathers of the Crow did not move in the light breeze.

FIRST SOLDIER: WHAT'S HE?
PAROLLES: E'EN A CROW O' TH' SAME NEST; NOT
ALTOGETHER SO GREAT AS THE FIRST IN
GOODNESS, BUT GREATER A GREAT DEAL IN
EVIL.
—Shakespeare, *All's Well That Ends Well*

"Almost finished. Doing okay?"

"Stings a little, no big deal."

Sarah made a sympathetic sound deep in her throat. "That's why they call me the Mistress of Pain," she said.

She peered through her glasses at the patch of Vaseline-smeared skin on which she was working. Holding the tattoo gun carefully in her surgically gloved hands, she let the needle travel over her customer's forearm. It made an insistent whirring sound, like a dentist's drill, which was only fitting, since her "patient" sat in a ratty dentist's chair she and Noah, her partner, had bought for sixty bucks at one of her favorite thrift shops.

But she wasn't filling teeth. She was filling flesh with colored inks, using pain to create beauty that

25

would last until its living canvas dried and withered in a coffin, or bubbled and crisped in crematory fire. A Japanese dragon wound its way over her customer's forearm, heading for his neck with a voracious look on its face.

She had told him she wouldn't have been able to sleep at night with the beast creeping toward her throat, but he had only laughed a macho laugh and said that he wasn't afraid, shit, it was only a tattoo, right? She shrugged. He was the one who had to live with it, in the darkness, in the night.

Sarah leaned back for a moment to relax, and let the man relax too. Despite his blustering, he had held himself tense ever since she had begun. "Gotta go to the john," he said unevenly.

She nodded and pointed toward the back of the ink shop at a curtain hiding a storeroom and adjoining bathroom. "Through the curtain, door to the left. Wash with soap and hot water when you're done, okay?"

He went fast, and Sarah thought he might be needing to throw up. She got them occasionally, stud muffins who weren't quite as brave as they thought. It wasn't the pain, which really was minimal, but it was the idea of something piercing their skin that sickened them. The bathroom at the Gray Gargoyle Tattoo Shop had seen barrels of barf in the two years it had been open.

Sarah screwed a jeweler's loupe into her right eye and made a slight adjustment to her needle. Then she sat back in the stenographer's chair and relaxed for a minute. Her gaze took in the cluttered shop that she was as proud of as her loft.

Sheets of flash, ready-made tattoo art, were pinned everywhere, and through the haze of Noah's cigarette smoke, the walls seemed alive with monsters. The dragons and serpents and panthers glared down from the sheets of paper on which they were caged, as if anxious to leap free and claim someone's flesh as their own.

And they would too. They would be reborn, like the stamp of the imp on Trinity packets. But instead of coming to life in someone's brain, Sarah's creatures would live on someone's skin. And instead of bringing death, they would bring beauty.

She looked past the neon sign buzzing and flickering in the window, out to the street. Their shop was the sole oasis of light in a shell-shocked block that otherwise boasted only desolate warehouse buildings. She got a glimpse of the rusted sign she saw every day when she came to work. It had read END CITY LIMITS before someone had crossed out the last two words and replaced them with OF THE FUCKING WORLD.

Maybe. But it was Sarah's world, and she had seen worse. Even the gaunt and rusting bridge that crossed the River Styx held as much romance for her as the Bridge of Sighs did for those who had visited Venice. Sarah had never seen Venice. She had seen Detroit for eighteen of her years, and then she had seen the City of Angels.

She lived as well as she could where she was, trying to ignore the violence and evil, and had even reimagined the bridge over the Styx as a tattoo, a skeletal dinosaur with a great arching back and a snakelike neck and tail. Two customers had actually wanted it, and it shambled through the streets even now, unless those who bore it had died.

Her current customer, a buzz-headed biker wanna-be, still had not returned from the john, so Sarah scanned the books on the shelves. Nearly all were art reference works, from the earliest cave art to the newest super-realists. You never knew what a customer was going to request.

There were also collections of pulp- and detective-magazine covers, airplane-nose art, and scrapbooks stuffed with ads and rock-group photos and logos. They still tattooed a lapping tongue every couple of months, and there was an occasional request for the rose from the *American Beauty* album cover. It seemed the Dead never die.

At the other end of the room, Noah was still consulting with a young grunge couple. They were prospective customers, but, from the edgy tone of the conversation, becoming less prospective all the time. Finally the buzz-head returned, looking a little sheepish. When he sat down, Sarah could smell the vomit on his breath, but she didn't say anything about it. She just asked, "Ready to get started again?" and he nodded uncertainly.

Without a word, she pulled a pint bottle of whiskey from under a cabinet and handed it to him. Looking thankful, he unscrewed the top and threw some down his throat. She would add it to his bill.

She finished the dragon just before closing time. By then the buzz-head was in a sweet whiskey buzz of his own, and was feeling no pain from the needle or anything else. He babbled a few words of heartfelt appreciation, paid Sarah what she asked, threw in a nice tip, and stumbled gleefully out the door, ready to show off his new ornamentation to the world.

Sarah sterilized the needles in an autoclave while Noah closed up the shop. "What was with the grungies?" Sarah asked him. The couple had stormed out of the shop an hour before, hurling a shower of obscenity at Noah.

"What a downer," he said in his Brit accent that Sarah still found charming. "That kid wanted me to tattoo 'If you're reading this, you're too close' on his bleedin' bum!"

"And?"

"And I told him we do tattoo art here, not fuckin' graffiti." He flopped down into the dentist chair and fired up another smoke as they smiled at each other. "Christ, I'm knackered."

"Beats pushing ink in Detroit."

"That it does, Princess, that it does." Then he seemed to think of something and dug into the pocket of his proto-punk ripped T-shirt. "Bought you a little present," he said, and pulled out something small and round that he tossed to Sarah. She caught it and saw that it was a handmade candy sugar skull. "They do 'em for the Day of the Dead," Noah said. "Nice, huh? Necrophagia, Princess. Eat the dead."

The Day of the Dead. She had forgotten. Tonight, October 30, was la Noche de la Santa Muerte. Soon the Day of the Dead would be here in all its grim glory.

"There's a fortune on the bottom," Noah pointed out. "Like a *mis*fortune cookie, innit?"

Sarah turned the skull over and read the strip of

29

paper glued to the bottom. " 'Life is just a dream on the way to death.' " She thought about it for a moment. "I like that." Then she tugged off the fortune, popped the skull between her teeth, and bit down. The sweetness suffused her mouth and made her smile like a little kid.

"You would," Noah said. "You Mistress of Pain, you." He stood up and stretched. "So wanta grab a beer, then?"

"No, I gotta go home. Haven't been sleeping much lately."

He gave her a patently lascivious leer. "Oho? So what's the dirty dog's name?"

"I've just been having some weird dreams." She pulled the needles from the autoclave and stored them. "Noah . . ."

"Mmm?"

"You ever dream that you're dying someone else's death?

The question seemed to stop him cold, but any answer he might have given was interrupted by the thundering roar of a motorcycle pulling up outside. The engine cut off, and a few seconds later there was a loud knocking on the front door.

"Sorry," Noah called out. "We're closed!"

The knocking became an insistent pounding, and a gravel voice cried, "Open the fucking door!"

The door was a solid panel, so that Sarah couldn't see who stood outside. She started to go to a window to look while Noah walked toward the door. "Look, man," he said louder, "I told you we're—"

The door burst open, hitting Noah and hurling him backward. The man who had kicked it open stormed in and punched the off-balance Noah right in the nose, knocking him to the ground. Sarah had no time to react before the man was standing in front of her, trembling like a furious bull. His eyes, decorated with dark teardrops tattooed by someone far less adept than Sarah, looked wild, and he ran a hand through his lank blond hair like he wanted to rip it out by the roots and whip her with it.

"You think what you did to me is *funny*?" he shouted into her face. He smelled of beer and garlic, sweat and anger. "Was that supposed to be some kind of *joke*?"

She knew him. He had been a customer, and she remembered his name was Curve, because it seemed like such a strange name. "Look, just take it easy—what are you talking about?"

"I'm *talking* about the fucking *tattoo* you gave me! I took off the bandages. *Look!*"

He ripped open his shirt, so that buttons ticked on the wooden floor like balls of hail, and Sarah gasped at the tattoo on his chest.

It was a crow, its wings outstretched in flight, rendered in bold slashes of black. Or was it? As she bit back her fear and looked closer at Curve's flesh, she saw, buried within the ebony feathers, what looked like two demons fighting with one another. The ambiguity of the image reminded her of the classic picture of the woman in front of the vanity which is also a skull. She had tattooed it once on a young woman's back.

"What *is* it?" Curve yelled, snapping her back to the moment.

"A crow . . ." she said.

"Damn *right* it's a crow! Now, did I ask for a fucking bird on my chest? *Did I?* Do I look like some kind of fucking *birdman* to you?"

Sarah could only shake her head no.

Curve paused after each word, giving the question deadly emphasis. "Then. What. The. Fuck. Is it. *Doing here?*"

"I . . . I don't know, I was just going from the design you gave me—"

A flare of red crossed her vision as Curve back-handed her across the face, and she reeled backward, bumping into the supply cabinet and falling to her knees.

"Stop it!" Noah rushed toward Curve, blood running from his nose, his right fist drawn back to strike.

But he stopped dead when Curve yanked an automatic pistol from his waistband and thrust it in Noah's face. "What's it gonna be, hero?" Curve asked in a low, grating voice that promised only pain. "Ready to kiss your limey faggot ass good-bye?" He hissed out a laugh and grinned. "I think so. I think you're shitting yourself you're so goddamn ready."

Curve's left hand dropped to the pocket of his studded leather pants, and he dug out a packet of Trinity. He ripped it open with his teeth, decapitating the imp. Then he held it to his nose and snorted up the powder, his gaze never leaving Noah. "Whoa . . ." he said, as if in awe of the rush, and then he pressed the gun against Noah's forehead, murder in his eyes.

"Over here, asshole!"

As Curve turned to look, Sarah squeezed as hard as she could on the plastic bottle of black tattoo ink. The

32

ink streamed into Curve's eyes, burning and blinding him, so that he screamed and twisted his head.

In that moment Sarah planted one of her Doc Martens into his groin. The sharp pain drove the air from his lungs and a chunk of puke from his trachea as he doubled over. His grip on the pistol relaxed, and Sarah grabbed it from his hand. She pointed its black muzzle at the black crow on his chest.

"Get *up*!" she said.

Curve panted from the pain, the air hissing in and out between his clenched teeth. Black ink stained his face and matted his long yellow hair. He cupped his aching balls with both hands as he slowly straightened up, his eyes glowing with manic intensity. An obscene smile split his face, and he backed toward the front door.

"You shoulda killed me while you had the chance, sugarplum. Be seeing you."

Then he lashed out with his right fist, smashing it into the neon sign with a shower of sparks and a crackle of electricity, and ducked out the door. Sarah didn't follow him. In a moment the engine of his bike roared to life, and the tires screamed as he raced into the night.

Sarah never knew a deep breath could taste so delicious. She felt as if she had been holding it for hours.

"You okay?" she asked Noah.

"Yeh." He wiped his bloody nose, looked at the empty drug packet on the floor, and shook his head in disgust. "Fuck me, wonder what they'll be snorting next." Then he looked back up at Sarah. "How 'bout yourself, Princess?"

33

She had been strong, but now she felt so weak that she could hardly stand. "I don't know. . . ." She felt tears coming, and blinked them back, hating them. She didn't like to cry, and hardly ever did. But suddenly it all caught up to her.

The City of Angels was vicious and mean. Evil possessed its soul, and denying it did not change it. She had told herself she liked it, even loved it, but it was a lie made for convenience's sake. And tonight the city grinned its death's-head grin at her and told her to her face that she was a liar.

"I just can't do this anymore," she said. "I'm so tired of this."

Noah put his arm around her and hugged her, and she accepted the comfort, pressing against him the way she had, as a little girl, pressed against Eric Draven, and for the same reasons.

"Come on, now, no harm done. Your stockings got a bit torn, that's all." And he tapped a spot on her black net hose where her knee poked through.

"They're *supposed* to be torn," she said, and then gave a little sob.

"I know, I know," Noah said soothingly, holding her. "Just a little joke, that's all. I just wanted to see you laugh again." He patted her shoulder and whispered, "Easy there, luv, easy . . . it'll all work out."

She hoped so. She truly hoped so.

The twenty-four hour locksmith was a good start at making things right. He arrived a half hour after they called him, and said that he could reinforce the door so that no one would kick it down again. Noah wanted to walk Sarah to her car, but she told him to stay with the locksmith, and that she would be all right. She hefted Curve's pistol in her hand as proof.

And Sarah held the gun as she walked down the dark street to her car. She only lived eight blocks away from the shop, but there were a few blocks between that she didn't care to walk in the early morning. The Galaxie 500 had cost her three hundred dollars. It was old and clunky, and burned a quart of oil a week, but it was also big and intimidating, and Sarah didn't give a rip if it got any more dents or dings, so it was a perfect car to drive in the City of Angels.

She always parked it a few storefronts away, at the end of the block by the railroad tracks. There was a bright street lamp there that she pretended kept thieves away. But the second night she had the car, the hubcaps had disappeared, and she had not bothered to replace them.

She unlocked the car, slid into the front seat, and removed the antitheft club from the steering wheel, glancing around her all the time in case Curve had come back on foot for revenge. When the door was closed and locked, Sarah dropped the pistol on the seat beside her and rested her head in her hands. It had been one helluva night.

When she looked up, the Crow was perched on the hood of her car, looking in at her through the windshield.

A chill went through her, and she pushed on the horn ring to make the bird move. But though the sound of the horn went through her like a knife, the Crow didn't budge.

She grabbed the gun, opened the door, and leaped out, waving her arms. "Get out of here! Go!" she cried, and fired a wild shot into the sky.

That did it. The Crow ascended unhurriedly on its great black wings and vanished into the night. Sarah watched it go and, to her surprise, felt worse in its absence than she had when it was there. The tears came, and she could not hold them back. She leaned against the hood of the car and cried for a long time, thinking of Eric and Shelly, and the Crow, and the unknown man whose death she had seen, knowing that they were all connected, but not knowing how.

4

AT LENGTH HE PAUSED: A BLACK MASS IN THE
GLOOM,
    A TOWER THAT MERGED INTO THE HEAVY
    SKY;
AROUND, THE HUDDLED STONES OF GRAVE AND
TOMB:
    SOME OLD GOD'S-ACRE NOW CORRUPTION'S
    STY:
HE MURMURED TO HIMSELF WITH DULL DESPAIR,
HERE FAITH DIED, POISONED BY THIS CHARNEL
AIR.
    —James Thomson, "The City of Dreadful Night"

And the Crow flew through la Noche de la Santa
Muerte, away from the outskirts of the City of Angels,
toward the bright and beckoning lights of its downtown.
Its guiding beacon was a flashing sign high atop a
monolithic tower. The message it sent was JESUS SAVES.

At one time Jesus might have saved from that tower,
but no longer. The Crow drifted down to the campanile,
a multistoried bell tower that crowned the decaying,
larger tower. The openings of the campanile were covered by a complex arabesque of rusted iron scrollwork,
like something the Spanish architect Gaudí might have
conjured up from an Art Nouveau fever dream.

37

The bird spread its wings to slow its flight and came to rest on a curved piece of scrollwork. Light glowed from below, and the sharp eyes looked down through the spiderweb network of steel girders that criss-crossed the upper reaches of the campanile, down to a dot in a box on a table in the lair of Judah Earl.

The tower still belonged to a lord, but not a Lord of Heaven. Judah Earl was a lord of crime.

Jesus saved, but not here.

What appeared to be a dark dot from high above was a stag beetle. The box it was in was only a few inches high, and the beetle could have scrabbled over it easily enough. But he was held by a thread attached to his carapace. This slim leash was tied to a heavy nail driven into the center of the wooden box. The beetle pulled at the thread, striving to escape. But every motion toward the edge of the box only drew him in a circle around the imprisoning nail.

Had he been concerned with anything other than escape, his coleoptera eyes might have seen the ruined palatial splendor that surrounded him, the shadowy shapes bound to the supporting pillars of the tower, shapes that, every so often, moved. The beetle might also have seen the heavy curtain of chain mail that hid a portion of the vast room, a curtain from behind which came the voice of Judah Earl, guttural, yet as whispery as branches speaking in the winter with tongues of dead leaves.

"Talk to me, Sibyl. Tell me what you see. . . ."

Behind the curtain, Judah Earl, sinewy and Byronic, gazed down at the surface of a circular table. His gaunt face was slashed by a wide mouth, and seemed old before its time, as though he had, since childhood, carried before him the dreams of his own death.

Next to him stood a shorter figure, whose face and body were shrouded in black robes and a cowl. She looked toward the table's surface, where blurred images of the crumbling city outside the rotting tower moved like ghosts. She looked, but did not see.

Sibyl spoke. "I see Death," she said in a hollow voice. "Death returning from the veil of tears. He has your name on his tongue."

Judah kept his gaze on the shadows cast by the camera obscura, a labyrinthine collection of convex lenses and mirrors that threw the images of the outside world onto the table. "It's finally beginning, isn't it?" he said in a voice fatalistic but without fear. "What mask will Death wear, can you tell me that?"

"I see the face," said the prophet, "of one of your victims."

Judah Earl lifted his head, and the faint wisp of a smile touched the corners of his wide mouth. Madness danced laughing in his amber eyes. " '. . . All my sins remembered,' " he said, longing for death with as much desire as the character he quoted.

Sarah sat in her bed, Gabriel curled up at her feet. In one hand she held a glass of wine, in the other a cigarette. She didn't usually smoke, but every now and then she just liked to see the smoke billowing out and feel the subtle nicotine rush. She was afraid that if she smoked all the time, the rush would disappear. This way, a single cigarette every few days, it was special.

But the cigarette tasted foul tonight, and she stubbed

it out and took another sip of wine to kill the taste. So many damn questions, but the wine and tobacco didn't make things any clearer. She turned out the light by the bed and looked out the window to the city beyond. Were the answers lying out there somewhere in the steam-cloaked streets?

She lay back, rested the wineglass on her chest, and closed her eyes. She wouldn't sleep, though. She would think, and try and come up with the answers she needed.

Besides, she didn't want to dream.

Dreams came true at the Second Coming, if your dreams were wet and leaned toward rubber, latex, leather, and the way that various bodily secretions glistened on them. Curve pushed his way through the club's forest of dancing, writhing bodies, ignoring the bare flesh on the raised stage, and the various indignities to which that flesh was being subjected. Time enough for all that later.

There was a bar upstairs where members went to let the sweat and the cum dry, and replenish some of their fluids. Curve lowered himself onto the empty stool between Spider Monkey and Kali, taking care to ease his balls gently onto the seat. The ride over on his bike had been a bitch, but not as big a bitch as the one who had hooked him in the nads.

The barrel-chested Samoan bartender came over, nodded a greeting, and set down Curve's usual longneck. Curve took a nice cold pull. It helped.

Kali glanced up from her drink, saw who it was, and went back to ignoring Curve again. He turned instead to Spider Monkey, who was clicking his way through a View-Master reel. He finished his seven, pulled the reel out of the black fifties vintage View-Master, and slipped it into his pocket, which was loaded with the round 3-D disks. But before he could load another, Curve put a hand on his arm.

"Spider Monkey," he said, opening his torn shirt to display his new tattoo, "what's this tattoo look like to you?"

"This a test?"

"Come on, man, just tell me what you see."

Spider Monkey leaned close and examined Curve's chest as though he were gauging the tensile strength of each individual hair. Finally he spoke. "A bird."

Curve sat back with a grunt of disgust. "Come on, man! Look again—*think* about it for a minute! Don't you see two demons? Two demons fightin'?"

Spider Monkey gave him a how-the-fuck-did-I-get-into-this look, and then stared at Curve's chest again for a good thirty seconds, tilting his head, blinking, and trying to blur his vision, before he sat back and shook his head. "Nope. I see a bird. A big black bird."

"Ah, fuck you, then," muttered Curve, turning back to his beer. Spider Monkey shrugged and slid another reel into his View-Master.

Curve took another long gulp of beer, slammed the bottle back down on the bar, and stared into its amber depths. Bubbles rose to the surface, and when Curve saw them, he thought for a moment about the bubbles that had come up from the water after they dumped that Ashe guy and his kid.

But he only thought about it for a moment, and felt absolutely no regret.

*Bubbles . . . she saw them coming out of his mouth and
nose, rising with the cloud of blood that was coming
out from somewhere else . . . must still be some air in
his lungs, yes, yes, because how could he be drowning
unless there was some air, some life left, and you can't
drown when you're dead, and he was drowning, oh
yes, bulging eyes and open mouth, and the bubbles rising, the bubbles and the blood. . . .*

Sarah sat bolt upright in bed, trying to scream, but
her throat was filled with something wet and cold and
rank. There was the crisp, clear sound of something
breaking, and she choked and coughed until she could
breathe again, and then she gasped for air, drawing it
deeply into her lungs.

The wineglass had broken, thrown from the bed

43

when she sat up, sat up to save herself from drowning like the man she had seen. The man . . .

". . . ohgodohgodohgodohgod . . ." she whispered, a prayer and a curse at once.

But though she was awake and free of the vision, something was still not right. The city did not cast its light through her window the way it always did before. Something was impeding it. On her wall, the shadow of a giant bird slowly spread its dark wings.

She whirled toward the window and saw the Crow perched on the sill, silhouetted against the lights of night.

"What do you want!" she cried, her throat tight and pinched. "What do you want from me?"

The Crow cawed once in reply, a harsh, jarring tone that filled the loft. Then it spread its wings again and took flight.

She leaped to her feet and ran to the window, where she saw the Crow, like a black pall of smoke in the heavy fog that had fallen on the city. The bird was drifting toward where the river met the sea, the docks.

Drowning. Water. The sea. The Crow. She knew then, or thought she did, and dressed frantically, grabbed her keys, and dashed downstairs to her car.

Her low beams parted the dense fog, and she thought she could glimpse the Crow flying ahead of her. Yes, it was there, low enough that she could keep it in sight through the windshield. It disappeared for a moment into the thicker mist that lay over the bridge crossing the Styx, but she saw it immediately when she came off the other side and turned to the left to follow its flight.

Down narrow streets and alleys it flew, Sarah close behind it, until at last it drew near an abandoned and solitary pier, a skeletal finger pointing out into the sea. The Crow descended at the end of the pier and settled on a weathered piling.

Sarah parked her car and sat for a moment, thinking that there could be anything and anyone down here by the water. No one was stupid enough to go to the waterfront at night.

And maybe because of that she would be safe. Why would even the predators come where no prey ever went? Still, she wished she had brought along the gun she had taken from Curve. In her haste to follow the Crow, she had left it in the loft.

She got out of the car and walked to the pier through the darkness. The distinctive smell of the ocean off the City of Angels was strong, a mixture of salt spray, gas fumes, and dead fish. Sarah turned up her nose and kept walking.

But several yards away from her car, she realized that her theory of desolation had been wrong. She thought she heard other footsteps, and hoped they were only echoes of her own. But when she stopped to listen, the supposed echoes continued.

She turned, beads of sweat gathering on her forehead, and saw a trio of vagrants coming toward her. Their pace slowed, as though they had been stalking, and were now preparing for their final attack.

Finally, ten feet away, they stopped. Their clothes were rough and worn, and they leered at her from their whiskered faces. The biggest one licked dry lips with a thick tongue. "You got sumpin' for us," he said.

She shook her head, afraid to speak.

"Aw, come on now," he said jovially. "You sure got

the price of a bottle on ya. That's all we want. I swear by God we ain't gonna hurt you. Just give us your money."

"I . . . didn't bring my purse," she said, hating how small her voice sounded, how weak she felt.

The big man's face grew slack, and his eyes narrowed. "Didn't bring your *purse*?" said the man. "Hey, you don't come down *here* without your purse. Without some money to give us. This place is ours at night, see? Not just anybody can come walkin' down here without givin' us some money!"

"Or *sumpin',*" added one of the other men. His mouth was black with rotting teeth, and his face glistened with wet sores. "You know, Willy? You know?"

"Yeah, Jacky, I know. *Sumpin'.* Now, miss, you got *sumpin'* for us or don't you?"

"I . . . I'm sorry, but—"

"Hey," said the third man in a brusque voice, pointing a fat, dirty finger at Sarah. "She got stuff around her neck, see there?" He telescoped his round head toward her, raising his several chins. "Looks like a ring. That a ring?"

Sarah's hand went automatically to Shelly's ring on the chain at her throat.

"Hell yeah, that's a ring," said the big man. "We'll take that all right. You give it to us now."

"She don't *wanta* give it to us, Willy," said Jacky, grinning with his decayed teeth. "So we could, like *take* it, couldn't we?"

Willy looked at him, his face sour. "I know what *you* wanta take."

"Yeah, well, you do too, Willy!" Jacky squealed. "I get just as sick of your dirty ass as you get of mine!

Now come *on*, ain't nobody comes down here looks like her, come *on*. . . ."

Willy looked at Sarah as if appraising her, then nodded. "Okay, fine by me. But I get the ring."

"I saw it first," said the fat man.

"Then I get her clothes," Willy said, closing the bargain. Jacky didn't appear to care what he got, as long as he got Sarah.

She had been listening to them in horror, and now started to back away toward the pier. The trio advanced upon her, Jacky in the lead, licking his lips, his hands extended.

Sarah looked around desperately for anything she could use as a weapon, but the only thing she could find was a jagged piece of board that had been ripped from a shipping crate. The weather had dampened and softened it until it was little harder than balsa wood, but maybe she could stick one of them in the face with it.

As they came closer, she was surprised to find that she wasn't so much worried for herself as for the man she had seen in her dreams, the one she had come down here to help. What would happen to him if she died now?

They were almost on her, and she drew back the piece of wood, ready to thrust it into Willy's face as soon as he was within range. Then she would run.

But just as she began to stab out with the board, something black and wide swept past her shoulder like an onyx-bladed sword and hid Willy's face from sight. The man screamed, threw up his hands, and fell backward, bowling over his comrades. For a moment the Crow hovered upon his face like a thrashing black rug, and then swept back into the darkness as quickly as it had come.

Willy's hands were pressed to his face, and blood was pouring through his fingers. Jacky screamed and pointed to Willy's cheek, on which his plucked-out eyeball lay, still hanging from a string of muscle.

The two other men ran, and Willy, his remaining eye half-blinded by tears of pain, stumbled after them, fight, greed, and lust gone. Apparently they were not used to such unexpected resistance.

Sarah relaxed her shaking fingers enough to let the board clatter to the ground and watched the three men vanish in the shadows. Their frantic footsteps faded away, and she walked toward the pier again, feeling safer than before.

The Crow was sitting on a thick piling where the pier ended and the water began. It was sharpening its beak on the rough wood. She listened to the delicate tap of beak against wood, the slap of water against the piles, and the thudding of her own heart.

Was that his heart? No. It couldn't be. How could his heart beat now? He was dead, and Danny was dead with him. They were both dead and under the water.

Ashe Corven, still tied to his son, bobbed and floated in the ocean's murky depths. Salt water filled his stomach and his lungs. His body and Danny's were caught up in a tangle of razor wire, a rusting remnant of a guarded cargo long since dispersed and forgotten.

Ashe's flesh was miraculously spared, unaltered by the ravages of the water and the bottom feeders. At the bottom of the sea, he dreamed . . .

. . . of Danny stretched out on the floor of their garage, painting a picture, his tongue pressed against the corner of his half-open mouth, concentrating so hard that Ashe had to smile . . .

. . . of the two of them having a water fight, rough-housing each other without harm, pretend fighting and loving all the time . . .

. . . of Danny sitting in his lap as he read to his son aloud . . .

" 'Midway through our life's journey, I came to my-self within a dark wood where the straight way was lost. . . .' "

Had he read that to Danny? Or did he remember it from his own reading? The beginning of *The Inferno,* wasn't it? He wouldn't have read that to Danny, would he?

Why not? He took him into the Inferno.

No. No. Dream again. Good dreams.

. . . and he saw Danny asleep, curled up next to him. He reached out and stroked his son's hair, and knew it wasn't right, wasn't just, knew that such things should not happen, that children should not die. . . .

The right eye of Ashe Corven, who floated at the bottom of the sea, shed a tear whose salt water in-stantly merged with that of the ocean.

And then his dead eyes opened.

A stream of bubbles rushed impossibly from his mouth, as confusion and pain and fear tore through him, and he looked with living eyes and saw the face of his son, of Danny, only a few inches from his own, swollen and gnawed by the razor teeth of fish.

Panic knifed his brain, and he surged backward, but the cruel barbs of the razor wire ripped into his flesh, and the churning waters rocked Danny's body to and fro, bringing the boy's dead face closer to his father's in a pitiable parody of an embrace, a kiss from dead and fish-chewed lips. The barbs slashed Ashe's clothes to strips, cut the ropes that bound him to his son, and dug into his hands and face and arms and legs as he and Danny thrashed together, until at last his hands were free. He kicked away the last of the razor wire and reached with desperate hands toward the surface of the water, swimming upward in a storm of bubbles.

As he rose he saw shapes in the shifting water, the shapes of his killers, walking down the jetty, marching him and Danny to the pier where they would die, and he didn't want to go toward them, but he had no choice. Where they were, there was air and life, so he swam toward them desperately, as though they were his saviors rather than his murderers.

He swam up toward them until their faces became clear in the water, and he knew their names—Spider Monkey, Kali, Nemo, and Curve. The hate grew inside him, and instead of cupping his hands to pull himself upward, he clawed them like weapons and opened his mouth, so that briny water filled it, wishing he had fangs to bite and tear them the way the fish had ruined . . .

Oh God . . . Danny. *Danny!*

Ashe Corven felt himself rushing surfaceward as though he had been fired from a submarine, shooting upward, a torpedo of hate and vengeance. He burst from the sea with a tortured howl, his arms outstretched, and grasped one of the pilings, digging his fingers into the rotted wood pulp and clawing his way up onto the pier by the sheer brute force of his will.

His exhausted body slammed down upon the wooden slats, and he felt the water pouring out of his lungs, roiling up from his gut, running out onto the boards and between them, falling back again into the sea. When it was gone, he pushed himself to his knees, and saw right in front of him a large, dark, irregular stain.

And suddenly he knew where he was, and knew what the stain was, knew whose blood had made it.

Danny.

He saw her again as if she stood in front of him, lifting her gun and firing without a pause into Danny's chest. At the sight he wailed, howling like an animal. The memory was more than his conscious mind could bear, and his eyes rolled up in his head as the whole damned, cruel, heartless, fucking world spun around. But before the lights went out, he saw a dark figure standing a few yards in front of him.

Kali? Or perhaps the real Kali, goddess of death, come to claim him and kill him again. He seemed to feel her many arms wrap around him, squeezing away his breath, his consciousness, as he reentered darkness.

Sarah looked at the man with a combination of horror and hope. He was coated from head to foot in the gray-white silt that covered the ocean bottom. Strips of rusty razor wire clung to his arms and chest like the self-torturings of a mad zealot. Just before he fainted, when he lifted his head and gave a shriek that prickled the hairs at the back of her neck, she had seen his face.

The barbs had cut him on his scalp and cheeks, as well as everywhere else, and his blood had smeared across his eyes and mouth, so that he reminded her shockingly of Eric Draven after he had returned from the dead and painted his face in imitation of the irony mask. At first she thought he *was* Eric, and whispered his name.

But when the man's eyes went to white and he fell back upon the boards, she saw that she had been mistaken. He was not Eric, but he was *like* Eric. His wounds vanished even as she watched, and his flesh became whole again.

Sarah knew that this one had come back the way Eric had come back. All she had to do was to look at his unmarked skin, and the Crow sitting on the piling to be sure.

There was only one thing she could do now. She remembered the moment eight years before, after the fight that had killed Top Dollar, his half sister Myca, and the assassin Grange. She was sitting in the bell tower with the wounded Officer Albrecht, and Eric's very last words to her had been, *Stay with him until help comes.*

She had obeyed Eric then, and she would obey him now. She would stay, and this time she would help.

Sarah knelt by the man, carefully unwrapped the razor wire from around him, then half carried, half dragged him to her car, and managed to get him onto the big backseat. She put her hand on his chest and felt it rise and fall, then closed the door, got in the driver's seat, and headed home.

Though she looked for it, the Crow was nowhere to be seen.

SOSIAS: IS NOT THIS STRANGE? THEORUS
    BECOMING A CROW!
XANTHIAS: NO, IT IS GLORIOUS.
SOSIAS: WHY?
XANTHIAS: BECAUSE HE WAS A MAN AND HAS
    SUDDENLY BECOME A CROW; DOES IT NOT
    FOLLOW THAT HE WILL FLY FROM HERE AND GO
    TO THE CROWS?

—Aristophanes, *The Wasps*

Ashe Corven opened his eyes again in the dusk of the
following day, All Hallows' Eve, October 31. The first
thing he became aware of was that his face hurt. It felt
stretched and tight, and when he put his fingers to it, it
seemed to flake and crumble away.

Silt, that was all. Dried silt from the bottom of the
ocean. But above him was no constantly stirring mass
of water. Instead there was a plaster ceiling, cracked in
many places, cracked like the silt coating him now.

He raised his head and looked down at his body.
There were only remnants of his shirt left, and the legs
of his jeans hung in shredded strips. As he tentatively
moved, flexing his legs, stretching his arms, the silt
whispered off in thin flakes.

Turning his head, he saw that he was lying on a cot

in a ramshackle loft. Dozens of burning candles gave a warm, orange glow to the room, replacing the sunlight that was fast fading from the high windows.

To his right, in the corner, he saw an altar. It was overflowing with religious trinkets, statues and symbols from every faith. Most of the candles were gathered here. Elsewhere the room was filled with mirrors, a number of mannequins in different but graceful poses, and numerous canvases stacked against the wall.

Of the two other living things, he saw the cat first. It was a white longhair, and was sitting on a bed several yards away from him. At first he had thought it too was a statue of some sort, but he saw now that its tail flicked, and its bright eyes watched him intently.

Next was the girl. She was behind him, and he had to sit up and turn around to see her. She was wearing a paint-smeared work shirt that might once have been blue, over a black, skirted bodice, and was standing next to a nearly finished canvas, staring at it as if contemplating her next move.

Ashe saw that the painting was of a woman lying on a bed, cradled in the arms of a man. But no, Ashe thought. Not a man, but a ghost. There was something phantasmal about the figure. He seemed to be one with the shadow legions that hovered on the edge of the painted bed.

Suddenly the girl in the work shirt stiffened, as though she felt his eyes burning into the back of her neck. She turned and looked at Ashe. Her dark hair was pulled back and up, revealing the perfect contours of her heart-shaped face. There were so many questions he wanted to ask, but he settled for the obvious. "Who are you?"

"My name's Sarah," the girl said, and her voice made Ashe think of her as a woman rather than a girl. It was calm and soothing, a balm to Ashe's troubled soul. But the things she said next were anything but comforting. "I had a dream about you. I saw them shoot you . . . and your son."

Oh, dear God.

"I saw you drowning."

Ashe closed his eyes against the words. He blocked them out, but he was not able to block out the sound of gunfire. Three sharp blasts that ripped into his back. He felt his body crumple, felt the pain that opened his heart and his lungs, felt the bullets rend his flesh. . . .

And opened his eyes in Sarah's loft, his heart pounding, that same heart that had been pierced and opened and drained of its blood. He leaped to his feet, reaching behind him and brushing the flaking silt from his back, where the bullets had gone in. At the closest of the many mirrors that hung on the walls, he stood and looked over his shoulder at his back, traced his fingers over the place where the bullet holes had been.

There were only three indented welts, scarcely the depth of pockmarks.

He turned to Sarah, shaking his head, thinking that this was impossible, but that if he was alive, maybe, somehow, Danny was too. He started to talk, but his throat was too full of confusion and fear and hope. Then he coughed, and asked, "How did it happen? How did I . . . survive?"

In the woman's face he saw sudden enlightenment

and great pity as she walked toward him. "You *didn't*," she said.

He could only look at her and shake his head, not understanding her words.

"You're dead," she said softly.

A short laugh of disbelief broke from him, cracking more of the dry silt that coated his face. He felt it drop away like heavy tears. "No . . ." She was lying. It couldn't be true, it was impossible, and her lie enraged him. To have gone through so much, and then to be lied to in this way . . .

He started toward her, not knowing what he would do next, and she backed away toward the kitchen area of the loft. "Stop looking at me like that!" he said in a voice of deep oceans and deeper terror, following her. "Stop *looking*!" Then he knew what was happening, and grasped her arms to make her tell him the truth. "This isn't *real,* is it? None of this is *real*! I'm *dreaming* this!"

The woman looked frightened, but she shook her head, disagreeing with him and with the only answer that made any sense. "No. You're not dreaming."

He pushed her then, angry at her and fate and his killers. She pushed back, as if trying to restrain him, and she was still talking, still saying words that made no sense. He scarcely heard them. He was near panic, and could only thrash about as he had thrashed against the body of his son far below the waters.

Then the woman suddenly pushed away from him, and before he could stop her, she had snatched up something from the counter and pushed it against Ashe. He heard the cat hiss and felt a cold shock that

56

made him gasp. When he looked down he saw something wooden sticking out of his chest, the soft place just beneath his sternum.

A knife handle.

"See?" said the woman. "It was the only way to show you. . . ."

His fingers trembled as he wrapped them around the wooden handle, and he pulled straight out. All eight inches of the blade slid from his body. There was no pain, no blood, no wound. Just a moment of shock as his flesh closed as quickly as floodwaters fill a mud hole.

Then this woman who had just stabbed him opened both hands in a gesture of friendship.

"I'm dreaming this," he said in a tortured whisper.

Her pleading hands came closer to him, and he tore away from her, pushing her back and running to the door. The locks and bars took forever to open, and she was at his side before he had finished, but he whirled on her in fury and she staggered back, leaving him to his task.

When the last lock was open, he threw back the door and pounded down the dark stairs, falling and stumbling several times, banging his shins and striking his head. But he felt no pain, and continued onward in his wild descent until he burst through the outside door and staggered down the stoop to the street.

There he raised his head to get his bearings. He would go home, back to where he and Danny had lived, to where he had worked, and he would crawl in his bed and go to sleep. When he woke up, he would know that he had been right, and all of this was just a dream, some monstrous nightmare. Danny would be there, and he would hug him and tousle his hair, and he would never, never eat or drink whatever it was that had given him this terrible dream, and they would be happy.

Awake and alive and *happy*.

Sarah watched the man from her high window. He stood for a moment, as if not knowing what to do next, and then he set off down the street, moving with purpose. The Crow was there again. It perched on a decorative pillar of her own building, and its head was inclined toward the running man.

Then it looked up at her, its brown-gold eyes intense, and took wing, following the running man, riding the currents that swept through the street.

It was time for her to follow too. Now she knew the answers.

Ashe Corven's body could no longer be torn, but it could grow tired. This night he had run several miles at a fast sprint, a pace and distance that would have collapsed any Olympian long before. Now nearly at his destination, Ashe slowed to a walk, making his way to a series of corrugated iron sheds beneath the arching span of a freeway bridge.

One of them with sliding double doors had a hand-painted sign mounted in front that read CORVEN AUTO REPAIR, ASHE CORVEN, PROP. Ashe stopped at the door and reached into his pocket. His small key ring was still there. He brushed the silt off the keys and fit one of them into a lock, then slid open the door. He stepped

58

inside, slid the door shut behind him, and when the rattling noise had died away, stood for a moment in the darkness, smelling the familiar and homey odors of engine oil, grease, and metal.

With practiced fingers he reached for the light switch and flicked it on. The interior of the garage glowed with light, some from fluorescent bulbs that ran the length of the room, and some from naked incandescents that hung over several workbenches. *A mechanic can never have too much light*, Ashe had always told Danny. He recalled that now, and thought about Danny down in the darkness, without any light at all.

Ashe walked aimlessly about the humble garage. He picked up tools and laid them down again, ran his fingers along the fenders and hoods of what he had called his "wrecks in progress," and sought to find Danny in all of them. He climbed onto the saddle of his motorcycle and tried to imagine Danny's arms wrapped around his waist, holding on tight. But his son wasn't there.

He looked at Danny's spot, the place where he had sat and played, but for some reason he couldn't name, he didn't want to go there yet. He wasn't ready.

He held out his hands in front of him and saw the dried silt, and decided to shower it off. Clean his body, freshen his mind, get himself ready for whatever he needed to do next.

A shower and toilet were behind a plywood partition in a back corner of the garage, and he stripped off his filthy and ragged clothes, tossed them into a trash barrel, and stood beneath the shower's hot spray. He stayed there just long enough to wash off the muck, for the water felt uncomfortable on his skin.

Then Ashe pulled on a clean pair of trousers from the extra set of clothes he always kept at the garage and finally walked over to Danny's spot. An army blanket lay spread on the concrete floor, and on it were several newspapers to catch the drips from Danny's painting. Canisters of tempera paints were organized on the floor nearby by color, and a chipped coffee mug held an assortment of brushes. A pile of heavy construction paper was on the blanket, and Ashe knelt and looked at the painting Danny had been working on. Danny's last painting.

It was of a man and a child. The figures showed some proportions, but the painting was crude. Danny had liked doing cars and trucks and planes more than people. Beneath the man in the painting was the printed word DAD, and below the boy Danny had written ME. A dark footprint soiled the picture, but it had no definition, and Ashe couldn't tell if it was Danny's or his own. He hoped it was Danny's.

He felt tears form in his eyes, and he touched the letters beneath the picture of the boy, the letters Danny's warm hand had formed.

ME.

And Ashe saw how it used to be before the bad dream had come.

Danny is sprawled on the blanket, working on the painting of his dad and himself. Ashe has rolled himself under the oil pan of a Chevy, and he looks over at Danny when he hears his son speak.

"Hey, Dad . . . what color should I make the sun?"

Ashe grins. "Blue."

"There's no such thing," Danny says, laughing.

"Well, there should be."

"How would you know when the sun was out then?"
Danny asks.

Ashe is trying to think up a silly answer when he
hears the gunshot from outside.

Oh no. Not the gunshot. Not the sound that started the
nightmare.

Danny's eyes grow wide. "What was that?" he asks.

The boy gets to his feet and starts for the door at the
back of the garage. Ashe rolls out from under the
Chevy and follows him, trying to stop him from open-
ing the door, from going outside. He knows what things
can happen in the City of Angels.

"Danny, wait! Don't look!"

Oh no, Danny, don't go! Don't look! Don't *see* it!

Danny has opened the door, and they stand together in
the open doorway, his hands on his son's thin shoul-
ders. They look, they see it. They seal their fate.

Spider Monkey, Nemo, Kali, and Curve. Another
man is lying on the ground. They are beneath the free-
way overpass. Debris surrounds them where they
stand in the dry spillway. Curve is holding a pistol.
Ashe sees the man on the ground move, and then he
sees Curve's hand come up again and fire a second
shot into the man's head. Blood spatters Curve's face.

The killer stiffens, and his head jerks to where Ashe and Danny stand thirty yards away, silhouetted in the bright lights of the garage against the open door. Curve's eyes pierce them from out of his bloody face. "See no evil," he says, and walks toward them. The others follow, moving fast.

He has no weapons. He grabs a tire iron, but in the face of guns, what good can that do? They threaten to kill Danny, and Ashe drops the iron.

They walk Ashe and Danny to a car, and Nemo says, "Why don't we drop them right here?"

"Never leave too much garbage in one dump," Curve replies, and Ashe knows they're going to die. But he can't do a thing, not with a pistol pointing at the back of Danny's head. He decides to wait, to watch for a moment when he can do something, grab a gun, push Danny to safety, yelling at him to run while he fights the others and maybe dies, but it will be all right as long as Danny gets away and lives.

So he watches, and waits for the moment.

But the moment never comes. They link their arms, father and son, and tie their hands and drive to the pier. They laugh and joke in the car, calling each other by the names he can never forget. Spider Monkey, Nemo, Kali, and Curve.

"I'm sorry, Dad . . . I'm sorry . . . I didn't mean to look. . . ."

None of us means to look. None of us means to die.

The muzzle of Kali's gun flashes, the sound explodes in his ears as he sees Danny die. He screams and screams until he hears Curve. "Nothing personal, sport."

Nothing personal . . .

• • •

A wordless cry of rage tore itself from Ashe Corven's throat as he straightened up in the garage. Sobbing, he struck out at whatever was near, seeing Curve in the rack of tools that he flung down and kicked, scattering wrenches over the floor. He beat Kali with the tire iron that he brought down savagely, crushing the fender of the forsaken Chevy. He kicked crazy Nemo when he toppled his motorcycle, and he upended Spider Monkey when he flipped over the portable lift and sent it crashing down onto a workbench that broke from the wall and splintered on the concrete floor.

At last Ashe sank to his knees, his face a mask of tears, and picked up the one thing there that still meant anything to him. Danny's drawing.

Then the door opened behind him.

Sarah stood in the doorway as Ashe Corven spun around like a startled animal and saw her. For a long moment he looked at her, and then asked in a voice choked with sorrow, "What are you doing here?"

"I . . . don't know." It was a lie. She did know. She had followed the Crow, and it had brought her here, to this man. Ashe Corven, the sign had said. Corven—so similar to Draven. Eric Draven. It was time to tell him the truth, to admit it to him, and to herself.

"I want to help you," she said. "I *need* to."

She walked toward him slowly, carefully but without guile, the way you approach a wounded animal that needs help but is afraid of the healer's hand. He didn't draw away, and she knelt by his side. In his arms he cradled a child's picture with two figures in tempera

63

paint. There were words painted beneath them, but his arms hid most of the letters.

Ashe looked at her, his eyes asking for help, full of questions. "Everything's so confused . . ." He looked at the drawing, and his face twisted in anguish. "Danny . . ."

She had to tell him the truth that he already knew. "He's not here anymore." Sarah rested her hand on his arm. "He was your son, wasn't he?" He nodded quickly, and hugged the picture to him again.

He needed to be embraced, and Sarah put her arms around him, relieved when he did not draw away. Instead he slouched against her, his head on her breast like a tired little boy. Ashe Corven stared up at her, his eyes distant, seeing something that she could not.

"There's no moon," he said.

She didn't know what he meant, but she touched his face to calm him further, hoping that he would rest again, but knowing that rest was no longer an option for his soul.

"You've been given another chance, Ashe—to put the wrong things right."

Her fingers ran along his cheeks, as soft and smooth as a child's, then over his parted lips, and up to his pale forehead to brush back the locks of hair, damp with sweat, that clung there. He had mentioned the moon, and she thought his face seemed like a moon, a bright expanse on which another face could be imagined.

Her gaze fell to the canisters of tempera paint that Ashe's rage had scattered. Several were within her reach. She pushed against Ashe gently until he was sitting up, facing her. Then she picked up the canister of white and unscrewed the lid.

Sarah dipped her fingers into the white paint and delicately began to paint Ashe Corven's face. Slowly the white covered his flesh like sea foam covering a beach, and she spoke to him restfully, softly.

"I believe there have always been people like you . . ."

Her fingers tingled as she performed the ritual. Over his cheeks and forehead, down along his chin, her fingertips drifted like the wings of a bird over a barren plain, casting a shadow of snow and ice upon the landscape below.

". . . restless souls trapped between the worlds . . ."

And then the black, dark as a night hiding lovers, ringing his tender lips, highlighting their blood ruby shade, circling his liquid, tortured eyes.

". . . searching for a way to rid themselves of their pain . . ."

And the accents, above and below the eyes, making them flare in a mask of war, a grimace of righteous battle.

". . . hoping that somehow they can be reunited with the people they love. . . ."

His battered soul seemed to merge with hers as she worked, even as she knew she must not feel for this man what she was feeling now. He was not of her world.

She was finished now, and he was sitting upright, his shoulders straight, his face looking into her own as she examined her handiwork. It was like Eric's, but unlike his at the same time. It was the same mask of irony, the legacy of the Crow, but it had been filtered through Ashe Corven's own unique pain.

"It's the pain that brings people back," she whispered to the man who sat before her, resurrected and now apotheosized. "It makes us strong again."

For the first time the dark saint smiled.

LIGHT THICKENS, AND THE CROW
MAKES WING TO THE ROOKY WOOD;
GOOD THINGS OF DAY BEGIN TO DROOP AND
    DROWSE,
WHILES NIGHT'S BLACK AGENTS TO THEIR PREYS
    DO ROUSE.

—Shakespeare, *Macbeth*

The Crow led him. It knew where he wanted to go, what he had to do.

The motorcycle roared through the night, beneath the Gothic arches of the freeway overpass. He traveled the lower road, away from the view of men, for his deeds would be dark and better unseen. Hellfire burned in his eyes, and justice beat in his heart, and at last in the City of Angels the night itself knew fear.

The Crow remained near him, its great black wings driving it through the night faster than the swiftest falcon's dive. Ashe Corven let it guide him, his dread cicerone. Ashe's long, black duster billowed out behind him in the wind, flapping like the wings of a fallen angel.

Finally the Crow slowed, and landed on a telephone

wire. Its beady eyes glared at a single building that sat humped like a tired, fat washerwoman at the river's edge. The bird's beaked head twisted, looking down at a series of pipes that carried steaming effluvia from somewhere deep in the building into the thick waters of the river. When the sound of Ashe Corven's motor-cycle sputtered and died, the bird looked at the man, who gave a sly thumbs-up and dismounted.

Ashe Craven walked toward the weathered building, while the Crow sat and watched and waited.

Spider Monkey absofuckinlutely *loved* the lab. Machines were so damn cool to start with, and when those machines made and packaged the big love of his life, they were even cooler.

Two big loves, really—great drugs and big money, and Trinity supplied him with both. Judah had made him plant manager, since Spider Monkey was the only one of his lieutenants who knew the difference between a camshaft and a caliper. Spider Monkey took his job seriously too. When he wasn't out on a job of wet work for Judah, he spent most of his time at the factory. Had to if you didn't want to be robbed blind, and Judah didn't take to that shit at all.

Spider Monkey didn't hire junkies, at least as far as he could tell. But just in case, he made them all strip anyway, guys and chicks alike, if they were working the lab. It was too easy to sweep a couple hundred bucks' worth into your pockets or up your sleeves, and if they were butt-naked there wasn't anywhere to put it. Stick any worthwhile amount in your mouth or up your butt or your snatch, and Trinity would soak into your mucous membranes and head straight for the brain. You'd have the screamin'-mimi heebie-jeebies for about ten seconds, and then you'd flatline. You'd be damn lucky if your ass didn't shoot flames.

He had seen people try it, and was always glad when there were a lot of other workers around to see what happened. There'd be no theft for months afterward. *Just in the nose, angelitos,* he'd tell them as they dragged the body out, and only as much at one time as a packet could hold.

The packets were what he was working on now, all alone after hours, just him and the big machines, ca-*chunk,* ca-*chunk,* ca-*chunk,* stamping those little imp bastards on the empty glassine bags. The imp had been Spider Monkey's idea. He had seen something similar as a logo on a little, squatty ugly car that his grandma drove years ago, when she had come and taken him away from his whore of a mother. Grandma had died just a few months later, and then Spider Monkey was on his own, but he liked it better that way.

When the old lady had finally stopped breathing, he had taken her money and ripped the smiley little bastard off the car with a screwdriver, then hit the road with it in his pocket as a good luck charm. He had carried it ever since. Sometimes he thought that he had whacked the old bitch as much for the little metal imp as for the fun of just strangling her with her own rosary.

Spider Monkey smiled at the memory and at the imp as he pulled down on the lever and stamped another row of the packets. Ca-*chunk.* Damn right. The imp had been good luck after all. He was Judah's lab man—all the drugs he could snort, all the pussy he could hump, and all the money he wanted. And machines too. Shit, life was good.

But his arm was getting a little tired. So he turned off the belt that marched the army of imps and plopped his ass down in a tattered, overstuffed armchair that expelled a light cloud of Trinity dust as he sat. He relaxed for a minute, surveying his domain.

The lab really wasn't much to look at. There were barrels everywhere, a maze of fifty-gallon drums that were stuffed to the brim with Trinity. The toxic fumes that wafted through the place had stained the walls worse than a juice junkie's drawers, and the blacked-out windows sweated a thick moisture that reminded Spider Monkey of the snot he blew when he had a real bad cold.

Equipment and machines were scattered anywhere they would fit. Heating mantles rigged with flasks and condensers rubbed elbows with vacuum pumps and containers of battery acid, paint thinner, and Epsom salts. Primo ingredients one and all. Christ, Spider Monkey had *never* seen shit that was easier or cheaper to make. The drug was a product of genius.

Spider Monkey knew it for a fact, since he was the one who had whacked the genius who had come up with the formula. Judah had told him to, and he always did what Judah said. Judah liked people who did what he said. Judah *didn't* like geniuses, since he was a genius himself, and two in one organization could be a real pain in the ass. Spider Monkey never claimed to be a genius, especially around Judah Earl.

He looked over lazily at the old TV set stuck between two barrels of heaven. On the screen, amateur bull riders were getting thrown and trampled. Spider Monkey's favorite part was coming up. Oh yeah, there it was. Old bull caught that drunk asshole right in the groin. Up and over he went, and man, look at the blood. Spider Monkey had paid a hundred bucks for the tape, but it was well worth it, the kind of entertainment he never got bored watching.

Ah hell, enough of a rest, he thought. Time to get back to work. He stood up and plucked a pinch worth of Trinity from one of the open drums, thinking that a little boost would be real nice this time of night. He snorted it up and said, "Whoo . . . *whoo* . . . WHOO!" as the powder jump-started his weary brain. "Oh my, yes, my little white *angelito* . . . you are so fucking *good*. . . ."

He looked back at the TV to get one more good dose of ultraviolence before hitting the press again, but the TV and the main lights and all the machines shut off. Only the panic lights high above stayed lit, throwing a feeble and fitful glow on him and the lab.

"What the shi—" he started to say, but the voice cut him off. It sounded like the dead talking.

" 'My mother was accursed the night she bore me and I am faint with envy of all the dead.' "

It took the length of the speech for Spider Monkey to figure out where the voice was coming from. It was behind him, and he swung around to see what looked like a slim, black leather Buddha sitting cross-legged on a table. The man or ghost, or whatever the hell he was, was grinning, and his teeth looked sharp and scary. His face was white, not just white like a white

71

guy, but *white* white, and there was black stuff around his eyes and mouth. Spider Monkey didn't like the dude or his voice one little bit.

"Tell me, Monkey," the thing said. "Does the corpse have a familiar face?"

Spider Monkey was pissed, now that he saw something to be pissed at. This was his turf. What the hell was this goofy motherfucker doing waltzing in like he owned it? "Who the fuck are you?" Spider Monkey asked.

"You have to learn to look"—the weirdo waved his hand in front of his face—"behind the mask."

He jumped down from the table in one quick, graceful motion, and walked toward Spider Monkey, raising his head so that the lights above could shine on his face.

Spider Monkey's mouth fell open and his eyes widened in disbelief. This goofo looked just like the garage dude they had capped a couple nights before, that Corven guy. When Spider Monkey spoke, his voice was as soft as it ever got. "No way, man . . . no *way* . . . we put you under . . . you and that snot-nosed little kid. . . ."

The dead guy's hand dipped into a drum of Trinity. He held it in front of him, and then blew a handful of the dust at Spider Monkey. Terminally spooked, Spider Monkey turned and reached behind one of the counters, grabbing for his emergency piece.

"Looking for this?"

Ashe Corven held up a familiar pistol, and Spider Monkey tensed for the shot. But instead of pointing the gun at Spider Monkey, the weirdo pressed the muzzle

72

to his own forehead. His grin grew even wider as he whispered, "Don't try this at home, kids."

The sound of the shot rattled the windows as the bullet smashed into the loon's brain. His head snapped backward, and his body slammed back onto the floor. Yes! thought Spider Monkey, forgetting for the moment that this same man had been shot to death before.

He slowly walked over to the prone body. His plan was to pick up the fallen pistol and empty the clip into Corven's head, finishing what the guy had started himself. But just as his hand brushed the pistol butt, Ashe Corven sprang from the ground, grabbed the front of Spider Monkey's coat, and slammed him against a table full of chemicals.

Beakers and bottles and retorts shattered on the floor, and their toxic contents splashed everywhere. Battery acid went into Ashe Corven's eye, but to Spider Monkey's horror, the man merely blinked it away.

"What are you!" he cried, really scared now. "What the fuck *are you*?"

The man leaned in close so that Spider Monkey saw the battery acid rolling down his cheek like a tear. "I wasn't sure at first," Ashe Corven said. "Now I know. I'm the boiling man, Monkey. I'm the plague of darkness and the death of the first born.

"All your nightmares rolled into one."

His hand appeared before Spider Monkey's eyes, and in it was a wooden match. Corven's thumbnail scraped the head, and it burst into a bright yellow flame.

Spider Monkey's bladder suddenly felt very full, and he held up a warning hand. "Whoa, man! This shit's flammable!" The match didn't move, so Spider Monkey relaxed enough to ask a question. "Look, look, what do you want?"

"The others. I want you to tell me their names, Monkey."

"Sure . . . sure . . . Nemo, Kali, Curve, and . . . and . . ." He wondered whether to tell who was behind it all, at whose order he had killed, but then he thought of Judah Earl's displeasure, and said no more.

"And?" said Ashe Corven, glancing to the side as if to decide which drum he would toss the match in. "I already know all the names you said, but who's the 'and,' Spider Monkey?"

What the hell. Kali and Curve would already be after him for squealing if this freak didn't take them down. "Judah Earl," he said. "He tells us what to do . . . *who* to do. He says anybody sees, they gotta die."

"Judah Earl," the man repeated, his face flickering in the light of the match. He nodded. "I'll start with Nemo, then work my way up the food chain." He leaned closer and his thin smile vanished. "Where is he?"

"Nemo?" Spider Monkey wanted to live. He talked fast. "Nemo's an old gash-hound, man. He hangs out at the Peep-O-Rama over on Deacon Street!"

Ashe Corven drew back, and Spider Monkey thought it was all over, that this fucking madman was about to throw the match. He stiffened for the final big boom, then winced as Corven blew out the flame with a loud *whoosh*.

"Congratulations, Monkey," Ashe Corven said. "You just bought yourself a fighting chance."

He reached into his pocket, and Spider Monkey edged backward. What would the sick shit come out with now? Knife? Gun? Razor?

A deck of cards.

Corven held it in his hands for a moment. The backs of the cards had some kind of weird design that Spider Monkey couldn't make out, but when the man fanned them, the deck looked like a black bird with its wings spread. "Special deck," Corven said. "Pick a card, Monkey. Any card. And hope it's high."

Please, Jesus, Spider Monkey thought. Gimme an ace and I'll believe in your holy ass again. He reached out, half expecting Ashe Corven to pounce on him, but the man didn't move.

Spider Monkey's fingers cruised over the deck until he stopped above a card that seemed to stick out, just a little. A force, he thought. Fuck that. And he chose the card next to it, pulled it out, and turned it over.

Jack of hearts. Not bad. He smiled tentatively at the man holding the cards, until Ashe Corven reached down and took the card that had been sticking out, just a little. Corven didn't even look at it. He just held it up in front of Spider Monkey's face.

King of clubs.

"Lady Luck's a bitch," Corven said. The deck suddenly disappeared, and the hand that had been holding it now held another wooden match.

"Aw come *on*, man!" Spider Monkey moaned in fright. "*Jee*-zus!"

Ashe Corven shook his head. "You're wasting your breath, *angelito*. Nobody's up there listening."

The next to last thing Spider Monkey ever heard

was the scrape of the nightmare man's thumbnail on the match head.

The *last* thing he heard was the explosion that blew his ears and head and body to pieces, and melted his good-luck imp right along with his bones.

Many people heard the explosion that killed Spider Monkey and destroyed Judah Earl's Trinity business, but no one was close enough to see it firsthand. If they had, they would have been treated to a hailstorm of glass as the blackened windows shattered outward, broad ribbons of fire bursting into the sky and roiling clouds of smoke pouring into the street and over the sickly river. If they had inhaled that smoke before the winds scattered it, they would have become very high and very dead very quickly. You didn't smoke Trinity, not if you wanted to live.

The only creature who saw the explosion was the Crow, whose feathers did not even stir from the blast. He sat clinging to a telephone line and watched the explosion and the conflagration that followed, watched as Ashe Corven walked out of the ruined warehouse, right through the fire, indifferent to the heat or to the flames that licked at his clothes and hair. Around him swirled thousands of the little glassine bags that had been hurled into the air by the blast before the fire had touched them. They fell about him like large flakes of snow, empty, light, and harmless.

Ashe Craven walked through the flurry of bags, feeling like he had never felt before. He was invincible. Nothing could hurt him. He had been stabbed, and had just shot himself. Then he had been in the middle

76

of an explosion that had ripped and melted the body of the man sitting next to him, and had walked out of the fire unharmed. Even his hair had not been singed.

It was a miracle. A dark miracle, for he knew why he had returned—to make them pay. Spider Monkey first, and now the others. Then, when it was all over, maybe he and Danny could be together again.

But in this moment, filled with strength and power and invulnerability, flush from the meting out of deadly justice, that hoped-for time of immortal reunion was far back in his mind. The flames said *not yet,* and his blood rang *not yet.* There was more work to do, much more.

Ashe saw the Crow spiraling down from the sky. It landed with the lightness of a milkweed pod upon the handlebars of his motorcycle as if to urge him on to the next killer, the next prisoner to be judged and sentenced and executed. Nemo, Kali, Curve, and then, finally, Judah Earl, the spider holding together the web of death.

The work awaited, and the joy of it. He lifted his head to the night sky, filled with smoke and fire, and laughed long and hard. His eyes were filled with tears, his clothes still smoked.

JUST THEN FLEW DOWN A MONSTROUS CROW.
AS BLACK AS A TAR-BARREL;
WHICH FRIGHTENED BOTH THE HEROES SO,
THEY QUITE FORGOT THEIR QUARREL.
—Lewis Carroll, *Through the Looking Glass*

The Gray Gargoyle's face-lift had been completed. The neon sign had been fixed, and the front door replaced with a reinforced panel and frame. Still, the freshening up had attracted no customers this night.

Noah sat at a small workbench where he mixed pigments and struggled to get a blue that would remain cerulean under the skin. Sarah sat at one of the drawing tables, a sketchbook in front of her. She was working on a rendering of Ashe in his black-and-white mask. Stopping for a moment, she sat back to examine it, and whispered, " '. . . that all the world will be in love with night.' "

"*Romeo and Juliet,* Princess," said Noah, glancing up from his pigments. "Hey, don't look surprised. I'm English, y'know. What are you working on?" He stood up and stretched, then looked over Sarah's shoulder at her drawing. "What's it, a harlequin?"

"No," she said. "Not a harlequin. A different kind of mask."

"I shouldn't wonder," said Noah. "Nothing funny about that bloke."

Sarah looked up into the face of her friend. "Do you believe in fate, Noah?"

He thought about it for a minute. He had always hoped that his fate might be Sarah, but he knew that wasn't to be. She loved him like a brother, but not like a lover, and he had come to accept that, even though he still wished it would be otherwise.

The simple truth was that he loved her. He loved her so damn much that he had been willing to die for her the other night when that doped-up bastard Curve had come smashing in their door. But apparently just loving somebody wasn't enough. There had to be something else at work. So he answered her question in the only way he knew how.

"Do I believe in fate? I dunno, luv. Seems to me it's more a case of fate believing in you."

He didn't know if she understood what he meant or not, but his reply brought a smile to her face, just a little one. She stood up, kissed his cheek like a sister, damn it, and then took her bag and said good night.

When she was gone, Noah picked up the sketch she had been working on and looked at it closely. The face looked familiar. It wasn't the curve of cheek and the grim expression as much as it was the mask that covered the face beneath. Then he remembered where he had seen it.

He had often had dinner at Sarah's loft, and had gone there more frequently once she had felt confident that he wasn't going to try to persuade her to be his lover anymore. Now they were good mates, that was all, and if the only way he could be in her company was by keeping it platonic, well, that was all right with him, and Plato could win the day.

But he remembered a ceramic mask in Sarah's loft that she kept either on or near her dressing table, he didn't recall which. He did recall the mask, and he wondered who it was who was creeping into her dreams at night, and on whose face she was imagining the mask that watched her in her loft day and night.

Again he asked himself the question he had asked her the other day: *What's the dirty dog's name?*

Ashe Craven sat on his motorcycle and observed the building that housed the Peep-O-Rama. It had once been a Japanese movie house, and a neon geisha-girl sign flashed above the old marquee.

The neighborhood it squatted in was one of the roughest in the City of Angels, but no one had tried to interfere with Ashe's passage. On the contrary, the gangs of toughs had drawn back from his bike as he maneuvered it slowly through the narrow streets and alleys that sheltered Deacon Street from the more respectable areas of the city.

More respectable, Ashe thought. That was a good one. All that meant in this town was that you said thank you to the corpse you'd robbed and murdered before you pissed on it and left.

Ashe turned his attention back to the flesh joint, the

entrances where guys were going in with night wood and coming out drained and weary, ripe pickings for the vulture packs. Maybe the victims wouldn't have as much money on them, but they'd be a hell of a lot easier to take down.

A huge neon eye beneath the geisha girl winked at Ashe, opening and closing every other second. It reminded him of a book he had once read about a hanging optometrist's sign of eyes behind spectacles that seemed to see and know everything that happened to the book's characters.

If you know, Ashe thought, you'd better warn your little buddy. Better warn Nemo. And then all the others. Tell them I'm coming. Death is coming fast.

Curve's eyes grew wider as he neared the Trinity lab and warehouse. His informant had told him it was bad, but he hadn't imagined it could be *this* bad.

Christ, there were scarcely two bricks piled on top of one another. The rubble was burning like crazy, and Curve was careful to stay upwind from the smoke, which was blowing across the river and getting whipped into the sky by the heavy winds that rushed down the Styx. Judah was going to be royally pissed, and from the looks of things, he wouldn't have Spider Monkey to take it out on.

Curve walked around to where the front of the building used to be, and there he saw, littered on the asphalt, the shattered black glass that had been blown from the windows. The fire was reflected in the fragments, and when Curve walked around them so that they lay between him and the burning building, it was like somebody wrapped an icy fist around his heart and squeezed. His balls crept up against his body, and his scalp tingled.

He looked at the glass, and then at the tattoo of the crow on his chest, with a sense of dread that kept growing inside him like a brushfire carcinoma. The glass shards that had been blown from Judah Earl's poison processing plant had fallen in an array that was anything but random.

They lay gleaming and glittering with golden fire, tracing the shape of a giant bird, its wings spread. Within the flickering outline, the asphalt was as black as sin, as deep black as the feathers of a crow.

A caw sounded overhead, and Curve jerked up his head at the sound. A crow, big and black and ugly, flew past a row of palm trees that grew at one side of the burning factory. Whether it was a stray gust of wind or something else, Curve didn't know, but as the Crow passed the trees, their broad leaves burst into flame, leaving them huge candles in the night.

Curve watched them burn, then looked at the outline of the crow, and finally peered into the night sky, into which the bird had vanished. Then he buttoned up his shirt, covering his chest as though it held a guilty secret, and got on his bike and tore off toward the tower where Jesus once saved and Judah Earl now destroyed.

He hoped that Judah wouldn't blame the messenger for the message, and hoped even more that he wouldn't learn that Curve carried the message, whatever the hell it was, under his very skin.

OUTSIDE THE GATE HE SHOWED AN OPEN CHEST:
HERE PAY THEIR ENTRANCE FEES THE SOULS
   UNBLEST;
CAST IN SOME HOPE, YOU ENTER WITH THE REST.
   —James Thomson, "The City of Dreadful Night"

"*Toh*-kens . . . *toh*-kens . . . tokens for the buddy booths . . . live girls, and I mean live . . . put in a token and they'll be your buddies, do whatchu want, letcha see whatchu wanna see. . . . *Toh*-kens . . ."

The Peep-O-Rama porn shop's Hindu spieler sat between two signs. The one on the left read REAL GIRLS WORKING THEIR WAY THROUGH COLLEGE and the other offered ONLY 25 CENTS A PEEP! The Hindu kept wailing his spiel like a litany into his throat mike, not even stopping when Nemo handed him a twenty-dollar bill. The words kept coming mechanically as he gave Nemo twenty tokens in return.

"Hey, raghead," Nemo said conversationally, "you don't even know what you're sayin', do ya, ya dumb fuck? You have a nice day now, y'hear, asshole? Oh,

85

and I really enjoyed fuckin' your mom and all your sisters. . . ." He pocketed the tokens and walked into the Peep-O-Rama. Maybe if the Hindu said something different one night, Nemo would say something different too.

He moved through the haze of cigarette smoke and cheesy surf music and nodded at the familiar, butt-ugly face of fat Zeke, the manager, whose temper was as short as the barrel of the sawed-off he kept behind the counter. Zeke didn't nod back. He never did. He just looked at Nemo, one of his best customers, with the warning not to misbehave glaring from his eyes, deep set in the rolls of fat on his face.

The heavy weight of the tokens rattled in Nemo's pocket as he walked through the shop. Twenty ought to be enough. Twenty tokens, twenty minutes of a pretty girl doing whatever the hell he wanted while he beat his meat, slammed his ham, and thrashed his hash until he was happy.

Nemo had a ton of euphemisms for jerking off. Since it was his sole method of sexual gratification, he needed to. He was a virgin, and had sworn to be one ever since his older brother, who had taken care of him when their mother died of AIDS, came down with the same disease.

Their mother had gotten it from dirty needles, or at least that's what Mike had claimed. Mike was good to him, kept him fed and clothed and even read to him sometimes. His favorite book that Mike read aloud twice was *20,000 Leagues Under the Sea* because of that Nemo guy, the coolest guy he had ever heard about outside of a movie. Before too long Mike started calling him Nemo and the name stuck. That was fine with Nemo, since his real name was Ralph, which he had always thought was dorky.

But then Mike got AIDS and it ate him up like crazy, and all Nemo's friends told Nemo it was because Mike was a fag. But Mike swore to Nemo that he wasn't a fag, that he got it from a chick even though he wore a skin. Before he died, he made Nemo promise that he'd never fuck any whores, with or without a skin. Nemo didn't have to promise. Seeing Mike die was so bad that Nemo knew he never wanted to go like that. And where they lived he didn't meet any nice girls. It was whores or nothin', even if you didn't have to pay for it. And he wouldn't stick it into a whore, not after watching Mike go down to a ninety-pound skeleton who had nothing but more days of pain to look forward to.

But he couldn't be a goddamn priest. He still got wood, and he had to do something with it. So he started going to Peep-O-Rama. Hell, there wasn't a thing to be ashamed of. Everybody else was there for the same reason he was. They *expected* you to flog the hog. Why else were the boxes of tissues sitting in each booth? And why else were all the seats plastic?

And the girls didn't care either. They'd seen the one-eyed trouser snake spit more times than they could count, even if they were *math* majors in their little colleges. College girls—that was a real laugh. The only college these whores were from was the College of Hard Knocks and Harder Titties.

Nemo passed through the magazine and video section, checking out some of the photos on the front and back covers of the sealed magazines, getting the edge for the main event. He went down a narrow hall to the buddy booths at the rear of the shop and found an unoccupied one. He squeezed into it, hooked it shut, and wiped off the chair and the phone handset with a wet-wipe before he sat down.

Then he sat for a moment looking at the metal shutter that covered the Plexiglas window, the token slot, and the box of tissues resting on the sill. Damn, but he loved to watch. The other night was a real ball-burner, when they took out that squealer and then that guy and his kid. He liked it better when they did women, but that didn't happen very often, and the kid had blubbered just like a bitch.

Nemo had gone home and watched the video of the hit afterward, and logged enough major wood to send him over to Peep-O-Rama. After all, he couldn't jerk the gherkin while he watched a kid get capped. Hell, he wasn't a pervert. But he had hosed the window in the buddy booth so hard that night that the whore on the other side of the glass had actually looked flattered.

Nemo finally reached into his pocket, pulled out some tokens, and looked at one. On one side was the open eye, and on the other was the same eye closed in a salacious wink. "No peekin' now," Nemo whispered to the token, and jammed it into the hungry slot. Feed a slot to see a slit, Nemo thought, and giggled.

The metal rose with a ratcheting whir, and Nemo's pride and joy pressed against his pants when he saw the woman. She was perched on a stool and was wearing a black bra, black panties that went up her ass crack, and a garter belt with stockings. She was better looking than most of the chicks in the booths, and might even pass for gorgeous in the right light.

The LED display was already counting down from sixty, the number of seconds he had left before the shutter would drop. The trick was to hold the phone and your dick at the same time while putting in the tokens every minute. Nemo was a master of the game.

He spoke into the receiver. "You got a name, baby?"

The woman looked at him, tired but ready. She wanted him, oh hell yes, but she did. "I'm Holly Daze. Do you want me, baby?"

"I wanta see some sugar, darlin', that's what *I* want."

Holly Daze unsnapped her bra in front and took it off, showing him an average rack but thumb-sized pink nipples. "Mighty fine," Nemo said through dry lips. "*Might*-tee fine."

The woman planted her high heels on either side of the window, spreading it out for him. She still had her panties on, but they would go soon, all he had to do was say the word. But not yet. Holly ran her hands up and down her body and uttered some tired-ass moans. He'd have to get her engine running, show a little appreciation for the goodies she had to offer.

"Right *on,* sister," he said as he unbuckled his belt and tugged down his trousers and drawers.

Holly eyed Mr. Willie appreciatively. It was, Nemo knew, one jim-dandy sight. "Mmm," she said, sounding at least a little sincere. "Is that all for me?"

"Yeah," Nemo said, starting to pull the wool on his bull. "We're gonna celebrate Christmas a little early this year."

She smiled at him. All *right,* now they were *getting* somewhere. "Keep doing that, honey, you'll go blind."

"If you're the last sight I see, baby," he said as he cradled the phone against his shoulder and deftly slipped in another token, "it'll be worth it."

Beneath the rusting top of Judah Earl's tower, another sexual act with no pretensions to love or even affection was taking place. Two women with perfect bodies, unscarred by the needle tracks that decorated Peep-O-Rama's weary harem of beauties, were grimly frolicking on a large bed. They were naked but for black masks with zippers covering their mouths and eyes, and an assortment of straps and bonds that left their most tender parts revealed to the mercies of the instruments of pain that they wielded on one another.

Several feet away from them were four video cameras recording their acts from different angles. And several dozen yards away from the bed of pain, detached and twice removed, Judah Earl lounged on a couch, watching the women on four video monitors, each of which provided a different but equally engaging view.

Curve watched the little drama and its sole audience for a moment, summoning up the courage to interrupt with the news that Judah would not want to hear. His key had brought him into the tower. He was the only one to whom Judah had given the privilege of entering unannounced.

Come in when you wish, Judah had told him. *I trust you with my life, because you are wise enough to know that if you betray me, your life will be far less than it is now. So I have no reason to fear you.* What Judah hadn't mentioned was that if Curve ever intended to betray him, he would know. Judah knew everything, thanks to that blind fucking witch.

Curve swallowed hard, cleared his throat so that Judah would know someone was there, and stepped out of the shadows. Judah looked at him, not at all startled, as if he had been expecting him. "Bad news," Curve said.

"Illuminate me."

"Somebody torched the lab on Manchester. Spider Monkey's a fucking crispy critter now."

Judah waved a hand dismissively. "I could care less about our late friend." His tone suddenly sharpened. "But what about our merchandise?"

That was Judah for you, Curve thought. Short on sentimentality, but long on efficiency. He took a deep breath and let it out. "Total loss."

Man, he wished he hadn't had to say that. Judah's nostrils flared and he stiffened like a panther about to leap. If he'd had a tail, thought Curve, it would have been twitching. But hell, maybe Judah *did* have a tail. He was bad enough to be the devil.

"He left a sign, didn't he?" It wasn't Judah's voice. It was that damn witch, Sibyl. Curve turned and saw her standing there with her hood over her creepy face, and wondered why he hadn't noticed her when he came in. How the hell could a blind woman move so damned quietly?

And how did she know so much? A *sign*. God *damn* her anyway. He answered uneasily, with a lie that he

91

knew would be exposed. "What sign? I don't know what the hell you're talking about."

"Yes, you do," she said, raising an accusing finger toward him. "You've seen it." She stepped closer, and the finger pointed directly at Curve's chest.

"You've been *marked*."

Curve batted an arm toward her accusing hand, but was afraid to actually touch her. "Jesus Christ, Judah! Why the fuck do you listen to her?"

Judah leaped from his couch in a movement almost too quick for Curve to follow. Suddenly the man was next to him, his clawlike fingers grasping Curve's shirt. "Because she speaks the truth," he said, and ripped open the shirt, revealing the tattoo of the Crow.

Judah stepped back, his eyes fixed on the image of the black bird. "Well, well. What's this, Curve? A beauty mark?"

"It is the Crow," Sibyl proclaimed. "And your enemy wears its mask. The bird of ill omen."

At first Curve thought that Judah was going to attack him, and braced for the onslaught, but instead his boss turned and strode across the floor, past the still-writhing debauchees on the bed, and swept back one of the curtains surrounding the camera obscura that showed him the seething face of the city below. He stared into it as though he were looking for someone he couldn't find.

"Let him come, then," he whispered, but Curve couldn't make out the words, and feared that it might be an unheard command to him.

"What?" he asked haltingly. "What, Judah?"

Judah screamed in answer. "I said *let him come*!"

• • •

Holly was coming, or at least that was what it looked and sounded like to Nemo. Her panties were off now, she was groaning away, and her fingers were playing hide-and-seek while Nemo's were shakin' his bacon.

The grease was just about ready to run when he heard Holly say, "Time's almost up, lover . . . better hurry with those tokens."

"Shit*fire*!" Nemo moaned, and reached out with his free hand. But the pile on the sill was gone, sucked up by the ravenous slot. He tried to dig into his pants pockets, but they were down around his knees, and his efforts to force his hand in just shoved them down farther toward the sticky floor. To pull them back up would mean he'd have to use his right hand, and he was so damn *close*. But to shoot off without seeing Holly in front of him, well hell, that'd be a *sin*.

So he tried for the tokens again, and his pants slid all the way to his ankles as the LED read, "00.03 . . . 00.02 . . . 00.01 . . ."

And then he *had* them, and yanked them out of the pocket, ignoring the ones that fell and rolled. He stuffed one in the slot, but it was too late. The shutter was already closing. It came down and stopped, putting a wall of metal between Nemo and his Plexiglas paramour.

"*Shit!* Shitshitshit*shit*!" With his left hand, he banged on the shutter, then stuck another token in the slot, and another. But nothing happened, and he punched the LED display, trying not to let his frustration wither his woody.

Then something clicked, and the shutter began to

rattle up again. Nemo sat back and started frantically to get Mr. Johnson back up to regulation size. But when he saw who was on the other side of the Plexiglas, his carefully maintained boner wilted like a unwatered lily after ten dry days on a grave. Nemo's eyes nearly popped from his skull.

It was the Corven guy, the guy they had killed along with his kid because they saw too damn much. And now Corven saw a whole lot more of Nemo, and grinned at the sight.

"Do you want me, baby?" Corven said, his voice dripping with irony and disdain.

Nemo knew he should stow his tool, but he could only sit there and stare, wondering what the hell was going on here. He felt dislocated in time and space and reality. But when he spoke, he could only say, *"You."*

And Corven answered, *"Me."*

Then the Plexiglas window exploded as the man in black slammed his fists through it. Nemo felt fingers clawing at his throat as he kicked backward, hitting the booth door and snapping the hook, so that he tumbled through it balls out, pants around his ankles tripping him up.

He rolled away from the door, tugging at his pants, trying to pull them up and stand up and run at the same time. The sounds of moans from the other booths and the booming surf music from the speakers over his head suddenly seemed nightmarish instead of familiar, and when he looked up to see Ashe Corven standing over him, he knew that the nightmare was real.

"Hey! Mime boy!"

Nemo looked away from Corven and saw fat Zeke

cradling his sawed-off as casually as if this kind of shit happened ten times a night. With no look but determination on his porcine face, he pulled the trigger, and Nemo ducked and covered, hoping the shot didn't spread wide.

He was lucky. The choke was tight, and only a few pellets stung him as he heard what sounded like a bucket of shot slamming into the chest of the man standing over him.

But when he looked up, expecting to see a sucking chest wound the size of Ecuador, Ashe Corven was still standing. He had been shoved backward by the force of the blast, but there was no wound, no hole.

Corven stepped right over him, heading toward Zeke, who was staring slack-jawed at the man who should have been dead on the floor but instead was coming to kick his fat ass. Zeke started to raise the shotgun for a second try, but Corven grabbed the barrel and snatched it from his grasp. His other hand gripped the butt, and he smashed it into Zeke's face.

Teeth and blood flew as the fat man fell backward into a display of videos. Nemo heard the crack of bones and plastic cassette cases as Zeke fell, the porno tapes raining down on top of him. Ashe Corven stood for a moment, apparently savoring the sight of his fallen foe.

Seize yer fuckin' day, Nemo thought, and started to run for the exit, trying to make no noise at all. But Peep-O-Rama tokens spilled from his pocket with a loud clatter, and glancing back, he saw Corven pump the sawed-off and aim it in his direction.

Nemo kept running, and the gun exploded, and he

felt the worst pain he had ever felt in his life as his left kneecap became nothing but a cloud of bone and marrow fragments.

Nemo wailed like a baby and collapsed on the floor. Ashe Craven slowly walked over to him, ignoring the human rats who scattered out of his way, the half-clad women who ran past him, the Hindu who popped his turbaned head in through the front door and ducked out again.

Nemo was his. No more chasing, no more games. Just a nursery rhyme that Ashe could not recall ever having heard as a child. Still, it seemed as though it had always been inside his head.

" 'One crow sorrow . . .' "

Ashe picked Nemo up and heaved him through a glass display case filled with sex toys. Baptized by shattered bottles of love oil, Nemo lay in a cradle of dildos, vibrators, and battery-powered vinyl vaginas.

" '. . . two crows joy . . .' " Nemo heard the monster say as he felt the toe of Corven's boot slip under his back. Then there was pain on pain as a superhuman kick lifted Nemo out of his bed of rubber and plastic, flipping him onto his stomach, so that his eyes stared directly into the nylon-haired snatch of a blowup sex doll. Nemo tried to push it away, to crawl wherever he could, but his desperate fingers brushed a switch, and the doll's prerecorded memory chip started to play:

Ooh, oh baby, I like it like that. You're so good. You're so good. . . .

The built-in vinyl vagina started pulsating like a

chewing mouth, and Nemo pushed himself back from it in horror, his mind going, not sure if the danger was in front or behind.

Oh baby, deeper, go deeper, all the way . . . oh, that's it. . . .

" 'Three crows a letter . . .' "

" 'Four crows a *boy*!' "

A boy, yes. Danny. And it was for Danny that Ashe picked up this piece of human shit and hurled it the other way, into the front counter, so that Peep-O-Rama tokens went flying and bouncing everywhere. One flew up onto the counter, where it spun quickly, showing Ashe both sides, one eye open, one eye closed, rapidly blinking over and over again at him before it rolled off the counter and landed on the floor, directly where Nemo was looking as he tried to push himself to his feet.

" 'Five crows silver . . .' "

" '. . . Six crows gold . . .' " Death said to Nemo as he looked down at the closed eye on the token. Then his own blood ran into his eyes, and he blinked it away frantically, hearing Corven's words, but also hearing the words of sweet sweet Holly Daze:

Keep doing that, honey, you'll go blind.

He kept blinking away blood as his hands pushed feebly against the floor, and his leg kept going out from under him as he struggled to get up.

Oooh, oh baby, I like it like that.

The vinyl vagina kept grinding with a sound of cheap plastic gears, and Nemo felt something grab the back of his collar, lift him again, and turn him over. He looked up at Ashe Craven, eyes clouding with blood. The pain in his leg had become so deep that he was beyond feeling it, but the air felt cold on his crotch, and he realized his pants had slid down again when he had tried to crawl away. He felt ashamed and scared.

But he didn't feel repentance.

" 'Seven crows a secret . . .' "

" '. . . never to be told.' "

Nemo pressed his eyes closed, and Ashe Corven saw blood pool in them. "Open your eyes, Nemo."

". . . Please, please just stop . . ."

Ashe knelt and, with the tips of his index fingers, pried open Nemo's eyes, wiped the blood from the wound on Nemo's brow, and looked down at him like the avenging angel he was. "You killed my son, Nemo. You took away the only piece of light left in my soul."

"We had to!" Nemo said in a tight, pained voice. "We had to! Judah's orders! Never leave any witnesses!" He sobbed for a moment, then said, "We didn't have a choice!"

Fury filled Ashe Corven, running down his arms to his hands and fingers. "We *always* have a choice," he said, and plunged his fingers deeply into Nemo's eyes, through the jelly, through the skull, deep into the brain.

The pain, to make what had come before feel like caresses.

Keep doing that, honey, you'll go blind.

Dark.

Dead.

98

MY SON, THINK OF THE CROW, IN HIGH GOD'S
NAME.

—Chaucer, "The Manciple's Tale"

Ashe Corven held his fingers where they were until Nemo's body stopped twitching, and Nemo's piss trickled out over his dead legs. Only then did Ashe pull his fingers out of Nemo's head and lift up his blood-covered hands. He turned them so that he could see both sides, lifted them so that Nemo's blood trickled down his wrists.

A door near the counter opened, and the girl who called herself Holly Daze dashed out. When she saw Ashe, red to his wrists in gore, and saw Nemo's eyeless corpse at his feet, Ashe knew she thought she was going to die as well. Lightning fast, he reached out and grabbed her wrist, not certain what his intention was, but knowing that he would not harm her.

"*No . . . please . . .*" She cringed at the feel of his

bloody fingers on her and tried to pull away, but Ashe touched her face and saw in one fierce split second—

Holly dancing, bumping, grinding, shaking her breasts and her ass, hearing catcalls and gross laughter, seeing staring up at her the leering, distorted faces of the men, their eyes and tongues and sweating palms and rotten breath all hungry and aching with want and I wanna be your fucking dog baby and bend you over and put you down and . . .

Ashe's eyes slammed shut as he reeled with the terrible vision, the bitter past and hard future. A touch had been enough to encompass it all, more than she could have told him in ten thousand words. When the pain passed, he looked at her, one victim to another, and tried to burn a laser beam into her soul with his eyes.

"If you value what you've lost," he said, panting with exhaustion from what he had seen, "you'll walk away from this place and never look back."

She nodded as though she were caught in a dream, but believed that dream to be more true than reality. There was conviction in the set of her face, and he hoped that she believed him enough.

He let her go, and she bolted like a rabbit flushed from cover, out the door and into the night. Into, Ashe hoped, a new life.

But there was no life here, and when he heard the sounds of a motorcycle's screaming engine and the loud bubbling grunt of a customized car, he decided to leave before there was more death. He had had enough, at least for the moment. It was time to rest, and let his vengeance build again. There was just time to do one more thing. . . .

As soon as he had heard through the network that there was a disturbance at the Peep-O-Rama, Curve knew exactly what was behind the disturbance and who was being disturbed. Whatever that goddamn black crow had turned loose on Spider Monkey was the disturber and he'd have been willing to bet his bike that Nemo was the disturbee.

He tore in on Deacon and screamed to a halt in front of the slime store, a car with Kali and two of Judah Earl's prime thugs right behind him. They all grabbed their weapons and headed for the door of the porno shop, Kali in the lead, thirsty for blood, and Curve bringing up the rear.

But just as he was about to go inside, he sensed something and stopped. He spun around and saw, sitting on one of the cars, watching him, the Crow. He didn't think he took his eyes off of it for a second, but by the time he had his assault weapon up, the bird was gone.

He looked around at the few pieces of human trash that hadn't been scared away by whatever went down inside. "You see a crow?" he demanded of one of them who looked like an old wino.

"A whut?"

"A crow, asshole! A big black bird. Right over there."

The wino looked where Curve was pointing, then looked back at Curve. Curve's shirt was still open from when Judah had pulled it apart, and the tattoo was clearly visible. The wino focused on it and smiled gently. "It jes' flew on your chest, bruthuh. You wanta shoot it off, I'd be careful, I wuz you. . . ."

"Fuckin' wino," Curve muttered, and followed the others into the building without a look back.

Inside, the place was trashed. A fat man was lying unconscious on the floor, his head bloodied, and near him there was a large puddle of blood and some other fluid Curve couldn't identify, and didn't want to think about.

"Nemo!" Kali called in a voice that demanded an answer. There was none. "Stay here," she barked at the muscle boys, two identical twins as blond and Aryan as a Third Reich recruiting poster. Then she gestured to Curve to follow her and walked past the buddy booths in the back to an open door that led to a dark corridor. She took point, and Curve followed.

As they passed through the doorway, Kali flicked a light switch, but no lights went on. Curve heard a voice coming out of the darkness, but it wasn't Nemo's. It sounded like a woman, but a woman in a box, or talking through a tinny speaker, or something. She was saying, ". . . Oh! Oh yeah, that's the spot. Do me, baby. Do me."

There was some light ahead, up where the corridor turned, and they went toward it, guns out, Curve ready for whatever madness that fucking bird could dish out. The voice got louder, and when they turned the corner they saw, in the glow of a red lightbulb, what was making it.

It was a sex doll. Someone had placed it so that it was sitting up against the wall, and in its inflated arms it cradled the body of Nemo. He was deader than three-week-old egg foo yung. His neck had been snapped and his head was hanging at an impossible angle. He looked less real than the doll.

His eye sockets were empty, and lines of blood ran down his cheeks and chin like tears. Curve heard the blood dripping with a soft splat on the vinyl arms of the blowup doll, who kept moaning:

. . . Ooh, oh baby, you're so good. . . .

There was something small and white sticking out of Nemo's mouth, and Curve knelt next to him and tugged on it. Nemo's jaw had locked, and Kali hit the side of the dead man's face with a clenched fist. There was a sharp crack, and the jaw fell open.

"You're so sentimental, Kali," Curve said without a smile. "That's what I like about you."

"He didn't feel a thing," she said without a note of guilt.

It was a folded piece of white paper, and Curve pulled it off of Nemo's lower lip. It looked to Curve like a snowflake cutout, the kind of thing he had made in school when he was a kid, before people started thinking it was more fun to use him than to educate him.

But when he unfolded it, he found that it wasn't a snowflake, but a cut-out bird, the same shape as the crow on his chest and the one made from the shards of blackened glass. His stomach felt sick even before he read the words written across the paper crow:

I KNOW WHY JESUS WEPT.

A phone on the wall rang, and Curve jumped. Kali remained infuriatingly still. It rang again, and Curve

103

looked at it, afraid to pick it up but not daring to show his fear.

Kali could smell it, the bitch. The third time it rang, she said dryly, "Are you going to get that? It might be the phone." Pissed, he snatched up the receiver and held it to his ear, not speaking.

"Curve." A voice spoke his name. It wasn't a question as much as a statement of fact, and Curve wondered how the hell the guy knew it was him who picked up the phone. Curve looked around, but there was no door or window nearby that anyone could be looking through.

"Curve," the voice said again. It was a voice he had heard recently, but he could not place it.

"Yeah?" Curve said.

"Do you know what they call a gathering of crows, Curve?" Then he knew. He recognized the voice unmistakably, and his eyes widened with fear. "A murder," the caller went on. "A murder of crows. Think about it."

The line went dead with a harsh click. Frightened and furious, Curve slammed the receiver back onto the box and then ripped the phone right out of the wall. He tugged savagely until the wires were free, and then threw the phone as far as he could down the hall.

Kali finally smiled, a thin, nasty whisper of a smile. "Bad news?" she said.

"Come on," he said, scarcely able to control his trembling. "We're gonna see Judah."

THE PRIESTES TAKE THE MEETE THAT IS LEFT,
AND GEUE IT TO THE CROWES TO EATE.
—Richard Eden, *A Treatyse of the New India*

Ashe took his finger off the switch hook of the telephone and let the receiver dangle. Then he pulled open the door of the phone booth and stepped outside. That would give Curve something to think about all right. Put the fear of God into him—or something with less mercy than God might have had.

He left his motorcycle behind and walked down a street, turned into an alley, wandering aimlessly. He wondered what time it was, and decided that it didn't matter anymore. It always seemed like night to him now, even if the sun was occasionally able to break through the dense union of smog and fog that cloaked the City of Angels.

Halfway down the alley, a figure appeared at the other end and walked toward him. Whoever it was twitched as he came, and when he reached Ashe, he pulled out a revolver and stuck it in Ashe's chest. "Sorry, man," the mugger said. "But I need some Trinity money, you dig?"

"Why don't you just sell the gun?" Ashe said.

The mugger laughed nervously. "Yeah, that's funny, man, so come on, hand it over."

"Stand and deliver," Ashe said, remembering some of the stories he had read to Danny.

"Say what?"

"Are you a highwayman?"

"Huh?"

"You rob people? You kill them if they don't give you money?"

"Yeah, yeah, that's right. I killed people."

Ashe didn't believe him. The mugger was scarcely more than a boy, and he was far too nervous. "Well, if you're a highwayman, that's what you're supposed to say, stand and deliver."

The boy cleared his throat nervously. "Okay, 'stand and deliver' and gimme the money."

"I can't. I don't have any money."

"Well . . . well, what you got?"

"I got this," Ashe said, sweeping the sawed-off shotgun out from under his coat and pressing it against the mugger's neck.

"Oh man . . ." said the mugger weakly, slowly dropping his gun arm to his side.

"No, no, give it here." The boy put the pistol into Ashe's other hand. "Make you a deal. Let's play some Russian roulette. You win, and you check yourself into a drug clinic. You lose, and you don't have to."

106

"I . . . I . . ."

"I'll even rig it for you." With one hand, Ashe thumbed the latch and swung out the revolver's cylinder. There were bullets in each of the six chambers. "We'll leave them all in. . . ."

"Oh man . . . please . . ." The mugger's voice shook like jelly.

Ashe snapped the cylinder shut and cocked the pistol. "And *I'll* go first. All right with you?" He held the pistol to his own head. "Well?"

The boy's eyes widened. "Hey . . . hey . . . you'll, you'll *shoot* yourself!"

"But then you'll win," Ashe said, and pulled the trigger.

The sound exploded in his ear, and he felt a slight impact as his head rocked to the side. Then he lowered the gun and smiled at the boy, whose eyes were nearly bugging from his head. "How about that," Ashe said. "You won."

The boy slowly nodded, his mouth wide open, as though he had just seen a miracle, and he had.

"Now, since you won, what are you going to do?"

"Go . . . go to . . ." the boy stammered, but the words wouldn't come out.

"A clinic," Ashe said. "You go to a drug clinic right now. Okay?"

The boy nodded again. "A clinic," he said.

"I'll keep the gun. Now, you just go on," and Ashe gestured with the pistol toward the mouth of the alley. "Go on," he repeated gently, and the boy backed away a few steps, then turned and ran.

Ashe slid the sawed-off beneath his coat and stuck

the revolver in an inside pocket, hoping that the kid would run straight to a clinic and that he would never see him again. He was glad he hadn't had to kill him. Ashe had heard enough gunshots and seen enough death for one night. Though he did not require sleep, he longed for it just the same.

And when he thought of sleep, the first thing that came unbidden to his mind was Sarah, and the softness of her arms when she had held him, the gentle touch of her fingertips when she had painted his face in the mask that the Crow had wanted him to wear. He thought of sleeping with her, her body warm against his own.

Then children laughed somewhere in the night, and the sound made him think of Danny. He felt a shock of guilt that he had not imagined himself sleeping while holding his son, reborn and alive, protecting him from the creatures of the night who had taken and killed them both. But no, he had thought first of Sarah, and he cursed himself for what he thought of as betrayal.

He saw the children now. There were four of them, and they ran a few yards away from him and vanished down an alley, giggling, their footsteps receding into the night. Then he saw what they had been giggling at.

A black dog rounded a corner from the street where the children had come. A plastic skull mask was tied to the dog's head like a big white hat. In spite of its grisly decoration, it looked remarkably calm as it trotted toward Ashe. When it reached him, it slowed, just for a moment, and Ashe reached down to untie the mask and free the dog from its plastic burden.

But the dog drew away from him, and trotted unhurriedly a few more steps down the street. It paused, and the hollow sockets of the skull's eyes looked back at Ashe, as though it expected him to follow. Then it trotted onward again, Ashe in its wake. It was, he thought, like following death, but he went on anyway, curious as to where the dog would go.

It led him to a small Latino church sandwiched between two derelict buildings like a flower between thorns. Soft music came from within, and a path of marigold petals was strewn on the steps. The yellow-gold petals seemed a soft carpet that led up to the open doors of the building. The dog scampered up the steps and went inside.

Ashe watched it disappear and wondered if he should climb the stairs and go inside. He didn't know what was responsible for his resurrection—God or the devil or something else of which he had even less knowledge. If it was the devil, going inside the church might be blasphemy. If God . . . well, he didn't know what it would be.

Still, he felt an overwhelming urge to enter. He had been brought up Roman Catholic, and had sent Danny to parochial school, though his faith had started to wane when his wife died. Old beliefs, however, died a lot harder than she had. He remembered the comforts that the interior of his own parish church had offered him, how making a confession had cleansed his soul, how, when he left the church, he had felt rested and somehow lighter, as if a burden had been lifted from his soul.

So he went up the steps hesitantly, crushing the petals beneath his feet with reluctance, knowing how he must look to the people inside, like a man wearing a mask, hiding his face from someone, maybe even God.

When he entered the sanctuary, he felt the ambience of it wrap around him like a warm blanket. He felt as if he had come home, and hoped it would be like this when he went with Danny to the place where they might both find peace.

Ashe watched, entranced by the glow of the candles, the scent of incense, and the sounds of soft and sacred music, all of which seemed even more intense than those of his childhood memories. Several people were scattered about the pews praying, some on their knees, some sitting, others standing reverently, their heads bowed. Ashe's church had not ministered to Latinos, so the lavish *offrenda* on the altar was unfamiliar to him.

Food and drink sat there, offerings to the wandering dead, with sugar skulls and floral garlands strewn about, decorating the gifts. Around the altar sat a number of photographs of departed loved ones, placed there by their families. Tiers of candles surrounded the entire *offrenda*. Ashe thought there must have been scores of them.

He slowly walked down the side aisle, observing all that took place almost hungrily. But suddenly a piece of the wall next to him seemed to move, and Ashe whipped about, his arms up, ready to fight.

Instead of an enemy, he saw only an elderly priest stepping out of a confessional. For an instant he looked as startled as Ashe. Then, raising one of his bushy eyebrows, the priest looked a question at Ashe, who relaxed his stance and smiled apologetically. "Can I help you?" the priest said.

"I . . . I'm sorry, Father. I was just watching. . . ."

"It is quite all right. Our doors are open. You are welcome here." The smile told Ashe the old man spoke the truth.

The priest walked down the aisle to the side of the *offrenda,* where he lit several tapers from one of the candelabra. Ashe followed, hands folded in front of him, trying to appear as nonthreatening as possible, remembering when he served his own aged priest as an altar boy.

"What is this all for, Father?" he asked softly, gesturing to the dozens of offerings.

The priest turned toward him and smiled. "Días de los Muertos. The Days of the Dead. These candles you see, we light for our loved ones so that they might find their way back to earth and share for a short time in the pleasures of the living."

Ashe looked at the offerings on and around the altar. The food appeared to be hearty but plain, and the other gifts simple. The ceremony puzzled him. "Father, what need do those in heaven have for earthly pleasures?"

The priest shook his head sadly. "Though it grieves me to say it, not all the dead are in heaven, my son."

The priest was more correct than he could have known, and Ashe felt a sudden urge to laugh, but bit it back as an old woman hobbled past him and put a small toy motorcycle in front of a picture of a child on the altar. She bowed her head, whispered a few words of a prayer in a voice that sounded like wind in dry grass, crossed herself, and went back the way she had come.

"Tomorrow night," the priest said, "we will celebrate. The people will dance, sing. . . ." He pointed with a spindly finger to Ashe's painted face. "Many will wear masks, you know."

"Masks? Why?"

"Some spirits linger here too long," the old man explained. "They become confused, mistaking themselves for the living. They have to be frightened away."

The priest paused for a moment as if expecting further questions, but Ashe had none. The old man nodded at him and walked away, but what he had said shook Ashe deeply.

Was he one of those who would have to be frightened back to the dead? More and more, he was thinking of himself as one of the living, and that was not so. Ashe was dead the same way that Danny was dead. He must not forget that.

Still, the priest had said that for a short time, the dead could share in the pleasures of the living. And there were other pleasures on the earth besides food and drink. And revenge. There was sympathy and compassion and even love.

Something bumped lightly against Ashe's foot. He looked down and saw a striped rubber ball rolling slowly away. Kneeling, he picked it up and looked for its owner.

The little boy was watching him from over the top of one of the back pews. On his young face was an expression of fear that Ashe could well understand. From the boy's vantage point, a strangely dressed man with a nightmare face had picked up the ball that had accidentally rolled away from him.

Ashe smiled reassuringly and held up the ball, then rolled it back up the aisle toward the boy, who stepped out into the aisle and caught it as it rolled up to him. Then the boy looked back at Ashe and gave a shy smile.

"Santa Muerte," he said, in a voice as light and sweet as finches' wings.

Santa Muerte. Saint Death. The words chilled and unnerved Ashe Corven, tugging the smile from his face. The boy drew back in fear as Ashe ran swiftly past him, out of the sanctuary, into the shadows of the night once more.

THE CROW DOTH SING AS SWEETLY AS THE LARK
WHEN NEITHER IS ATTENDED.
—Shakespeare, *The Merchant of Venice*

Sarah sat back and looked at the canvas searchingly. It was closer now. She had made a few changes here and there, most notably in the faces of the woman and the man in whose arms she lay. The ghostly legions around the couple were the same. The dead never change, she thought.

Gabriel stood suddenly, his back arching. His hair stood on end, and he gazed with wide, slitted eyes toward the half-moon window. Sarah didn't look. She had always heard that cats were blessed—or cursed— with the ability to see ghosts, and many times Gabriel had stared at nothing Sarah could see while his fur became ruffled and a low growl rumbled in his throat.

The first time it happened had been late one night after she had come home from the Gray Gargoyle.

Sarah had automatically turned to look toward the window and, from the corner of her eye, had seen something vanish just before it came into her direct gaze. She had only had a glimpse of it, but what she had seen made her certain she wished to see no more. It was in the shape of a human, gray white, and its eyes were black hollows in its head.

That was all she could remember, and could not forget. Gabriel had done the same spooky move several times since, and Sarah would not turn around again until, after several seconds, the cat returned to its usual sedate self.

But now Gabriel did something he had never done before. His fur settled down, he sat up normally, and he purred at whatever he still saw in the window. Sarah turned to look, slowly, lest some horror be waiting to terrify her. At first, she thought that what crouched there was a gargoyle in silhouette, but then, to her relief and joy, she saw Ashe Corven perched on the sill.

She didn't know what to say, so chose the obvious. "You came back. . . ."

Ashe smiled. "Heaven wouldn't have me. And hell was afraid I'd take the place over."

She knew it couldn't be true, but also knew that there was more in those few words than he was actually telling her. "I'm glad you're all right," she said.

Ashe dropped into the loft as gently as the cat that padded up to welcome him. He rubbed it behind the ears, then picked it up and petted it. He didn't look at her when he said, "I needed to see you again."

Gabriel purred more loudly, and Ashe set the cat down on a soft chair. He still didn't look at Sarah, but walked over to the painting she had been examining when he arrived. For a long time he looked at the face of the woman in her lover's arms. Then he reached out, and his fingers brushed the painted woman's face. "She looks like you," he said.

She did, Sarah thought. She hadn't created the resemblance purposely, but he was right. It was there. She looked at her face shining back at her from out of one of her many mirrors. "I guess I paint what I see," she said.

Ashe Corven turned from the painting and walked toward her. As he approached, she noticed something the color of rust that had dried under his nails and coated the hair on his wrists, but she did not mention it to him. He had come back for blood, and she would not fault him for it any more than she had faulted Eric Draven.

Ashe pointed to Sarah's throat, where her ankh and Shelly's engagement ring were dangling from the gold chain. "They're very pretty. What are they?"

"The one is an ankh, the symbol of immortality. The other's an engagement ring."

"Oh." He looked uncomfortable. "Are you engaged?"

"It belonged to a friend," she said. The ring seemed to pull down on her neck, heavy with loss.

He spread his hands, as if asking for more information. "So where is she now?"

"In a better place," Sarah said. She slipped a finger through the ring and turned it around nervously. "With the man who gave it to her. They're both gone now. At

117

peace." She looked up at Ashe. "The Crow brought him back. Like it brought you back."

"Who was your friend? What happened to him?" Ashe asked, sitting down across from her.

She put her head back and looked up at the ceiling. "It was a long time ago. In Detroit. I was just a skatepunk street kid at the time. My life was about as empty as you could get. But Eric and Shelly helped to fill it up.

"Eric—that was his name, Eric Draven, and Shelly was his fiancée. He played in a rock band, and they would take me up to their apartment. It was a loft, kind of like this one. They'd feed me and talk to me and stuff."

"What about your family?" Ashe asked.

"I didn't have much of one. Darla . . ." Sarah gave an uncomfortable laugh. "That's what I called her. She didn't like to be called Mother, she said it made her feel too old. Anyway, she was the classic substance abuser." Her face darkened. "She taught me a lot. Anyway, she wasn't much of a parent. Hung out and slept with a variety of scum. So when Eric and Shelly offered me a little companionship, well, I took it.

"But then they killed them."

"Who?"

"Top Dollar's men. He was the local crime boss, sort of like Judah Earl is around here." She noticed Ashe stiffen at the name. "He had them killed. On Devil's Night, the night before Halloween, when they set fires all over the city. It broke my heart. But Eric came back. He loved Shelly so much that his pain and his loss were so strong that Death couldn't hold them. Or maybe Death decided he couldn't have Eric in his land until things were set right.

"So the Crow brought Eric back from the grave. I know. I saw him, I talked to him." She held up the engagement ring. "He gave me this."

"And did he . . . set things right?" Ashe whispered.

She nodded. "He killed them all. Top Dollar, T-Bird, Skank, Funboy, Tin-Tin, and a whole lot more who got in his way. Then he could rest. Then he could be with Shelly."

"He . . . died again?"

Sarah looked at him kindly, trying to make him understand. "He was always dead, Ashe. He just went back to where he belonged."

"And what happened to you?"

She smiled. "Darla was cool for a while. What she saw Eric do put the fear of God—or the devil—into her. But after a while she drifted back, became what she'd been before. And I lost my mother again. A year later I lost her for good. She OD'd. I found her lying naked in the kitchen. The guy she had been with disappeared. Eric and Shelly were gone. So I was really on my own. Except for Gabriel." She reached over and rubbed the cat's ears. "He belonged to Eric and Shelly. Now he belongs to me. He was the only thing I had for a long time. The only being that kept me from . . . going over the edge."

When she looked at Ashe, she noticed his gaze was fixed on her forearm and wrist. Her history was there for everyone to see, a map of her past written in scars and track marks. They had faded with the years, but were still there for those who knew how to read them.

"Yes," she said, self-consciously crossing her arms on her chest. "They show a lot, don't they?" But she looked directly into his eyes, rising to the challenge. "But that's the past. It's like Eric said in one of his songs, it can't rain all the time. I left Detroit because I wanted it to stop raining. I wanted to leave that past behind me."

She passed a hand across her eyes, struggling to put it into words. "The problem is, I think I see the future, and it isn't that much better. The other night there was this girl . . . she was living in a stairwell, sleeping on cardboard boxes. She told me her name was Grace. A Trinity junkie, just surviving from day to day. Skinny and pale and sad . . . and she reminded me so much of the way that I was in Detroit after Darla died."

Sarah gave a low laugh, remembering the girl. "Poor little thing. And I do mean poor—she had absolutely nothing. Just a little purple bag with a beaded happy face sewn on it. Nothing in it, not a damn thing, but she held on to that bag like . . . like it was her last chance at life. I guess it was all she had left from whatever miserable excuse for a childhood she had.

"She let me buy her something to eat, and we talked, and I gave her some money. I told her about what had happened to me, what I had to do to survive, and then what I had done"—Sarah gestured around her, at her loft, and the life she had made—"to *live*. I made her promise not to spend the money on drugs, and told her about a shelter where she could get help.

"She cried, and said she would go to it. I watched her walk away in the right direction, but I don't know if she stayed on it or not. Probably not.

"Oh God," she said, shaking her head. "I don't want it to end badly for her. But so often it does. And I look into my future, and I know how it ends. In blood. And violence. I don't want to be a part of it anymore, but I don't think I can escape it, any more than you can. . . ."

She left it unfinished. He had his own problems, and she had already burdened him with enough of hers. "What about you?" she asked him. "Tell me what happened. Please. I want to know."

Ashe looked back at the half-moon window through which he had come in, then at the woman who had told him her sad story. She had trusted him enough to confide in him, and she had known why he was there to begin with. If he could not talk to her, there was no one in this land of the living that he could talk to.

Besides, he wanted to tell her what had happened. He had not talked intimately to a woman in years, but he wanted to talk to Sarah. There was something about her that drew him. She was warm and strong, and she looked at him as though she cared.

"Danny's mother left after he was born," he began. "She was a drug addict, like your mother. She's dead now too."

Sarah nodded. "Small world," she said, without a trace of humor.

Small world, and a sad one. "We got married too young. She wasn't ready to settle down, too free a spirit. But I talked her into it. She was never really happy with the marriage. She started hanging out with . . . bad people, and soon she was high all the time. When she got pregnant, I made her get off the drugs, practically put her under lock and key, so it wouldn't hurt the baby. She hated me for it. Soon as Danny arrived, she took off. The police called me six months later. They found her in a hotel." He cleared his throat. "Same condition as your mother—naked and dead of a heroin overdose."

"Forgive me, but if she was that crazy," Sarah asked, "why did she marry you in the first place?"

"She liked speed. I always had fast cars and bikes. It was my hobby and my passion. But after we got married and I opened my own garage, well, then it was different. It was work, a job. Something boring. I think she'd have been happier if I'd been a professional killer." He felt a bitter smile twist his mouth. "Maybe she'd be happy with me now.

"Anyway, after she was gone, Danny was all I had. He grew up in the garage. I took care of him there rather than send him to day care because, first, I couldn't afford it, and second . . . well, I just loved him. I loved having him around, teaching him to talk and read." Ashe smiled. "He loved to draw best of all. He'd lie there for hours and draw the cars and motorcycles I was working on, and we'd talk and I'd tell him everything that I knew. He was a bright kid, very smart.

"When he was old enough, I sent him to parochial school. I didn't have much faith left myself, but it was something that I wanted for him. Does that make any sense?"

"I think," Sarah said, "that the things we want most for children are what we don't have ourselves."

"Yeah. I guess you're right. Anyway, he really took to it. The sisters loved him, and he loved school. Every day after school, he'd come back to the garage and sit and do his homework while I finished working on the cars. Then maybe we'd go home—this little apartment. Nothing much there except some beds and chairs, a kitchen and a TV. Most of the time we spent in the garage. That was really home.

"That's where we were . . . when it happened. We heard a shot, Danny opened the back door, and they saw us seeing them. And that was it. They took us to the dock, and they shot Danny, and then they shot me. And they threw us into the water.

"And we died."

Sarah felt an ache for a cigarette, and took the pack from her purse. Only a few remained, and they were stale and dry. But she lit one, and took a long drag, reveling in the harsh, acrid taste of the smoke as it poured out of her mouth. It was like breathing out grief.

"And now," she asked, "are you doing what you set out to do? What you came back for?"

"Yes," he said, as though it gave him no great joy. But then his tone grew angry. "It wasn't right, what happened to Danny. He shouldn't have died like that."

"No," she said. "He shouldn't." She put her hand on his. "It was very wrong."

Ashe turned his hand upward so that his fingers wrapped around hers. "You know things, Sarah, don't you? You've seen . . . what's happening to me now, when it happened to Eric."

Sarah rubbed the engagement ring again. "Yes. I have."

"I'm going to finish what I'm supposed to do here. But what happens to me when I do?"

"You go back," she said quietly.

"And what if . . ." The pressure of his fingers increased slightly. "What if I don't *want* to go back?"

She looked away from his pleading eyes, and gently drew back her hand. "Then you're damned."

Except for the mirrors, the loft was full of furniture and fabrics and canvases, soft surfaces all. But the word, *damned,* seemed to echo and reecho in Sarah's ears for a long time, as though it rang off of canyons, and down deep abysses, and was shouted from atop high towers made of iron.

In the tower, they watched and listened when the dead man told them to:

Listen to me, please! He's just a kid.

"That's the guy, man," said Curve. "That's his voice!"

Let him go, he can't hurt you! He doesn't even know who you are.

"I heard him on the phone, goddamn it!"

Kill me, but please don't—

They watched the video monitor as Kali shot the boy in the chest and the father screamed. Neither Curve nor Kali nor Judah Earl winced when the bullet went in. Judah's face remained quietly intent, Kali's unmoving and stolid, Curve's edged with panic. Nearby, Sibyl stood, her cowled face turned away from the screen.

They continued to watch as Curve shot Ashe Corven, and kept watching and listening as the bodies fell

124

into the water, and Corven's face slowly sank beneath the surface, his eyes still open, lit brightly by Nemo's camcorder light.

It had nearly vanished from sight when Curve slapped the button on the VCR to stop the tape, but he hit the wrong one, so that it only froze the image. Two eyes looked up through the murk like a water spirit, and Curve shuddered and turned away.

"That was him!" he insisted. "It was that son-of-a-bitch we dumped off the pier, Judah, I *know* it!" He whirled away, dug a packet of Trinity from his pants pocket, ripped it open, and snorted it up. Shit, he thought, just when he needed it most, it had about as much effect as fucking baby powder.

"I thought you killed him," said Judah.

"I *did*!" Curve started pacing up and down. His gut felt like birds were fluttering around inside it. "Christ, you saw it! I shot him three fucking times, okay? His eyes didn't even blink when he went in the water, you saw it! He was *dead*!"

"He's a ghost," said Kali in such a flat tone that Curve couldn't tell if she was serious or just jiving him.

"Bullshit! No such thing as ghosts," Curve said, not at all sure. Maybe the bastard *was* a ghost, but he'd be damned if he'd agree with Kali.

"Then who killed Spider Monkey and Nemo?" she said pointedly. "And who trashed the factory and the Peep-O-Rama?"

Curve's pacing increased in speed. Now it felt like a crow was flapping around inside his guts. A crow. That was the key, and the thing that scared the shit out of him. "I don't know," Curve said, "if he's a ghost or *what* he is. But I do know, he's fucking with us. And the Crow's his symbol, right? That means I'm marked, man, that means he's coming for *me* now!"

Kali gave a derisive snort of laughter. "I thought you said you didn't believe in that stuff."

Jesus *Christ,* Curve didn't *need* this shit. He turned on the bitch, ready to backhand her, but in a movement faster than he could even follow, Kali had drawn one of her katanas, and Curve found its deadly blade only inches from his face.

He backed away, bristling, but not wanting to die yet. "Look, you want to tell yourselves some bullshit fairy tales, that's your business. But I'm not gonna sit here with a fucking *target* on my chest!" He pounded a fist against his tattoo, and wished it were Kali's face—or Ashe Corven's life. "I'm going to take this motherfucker out!"

"No."

The word was spoken quietly, and Curve, along with the others, turned to Sibyl, whose back was still turned to them. " 'No'?" Curve said. "What do you mean, no?"

"You won't stop him with bullets or knives," Sibyl said, and her voice, as always, gave Curve the holy creeps. "He doesn't feel pain. He doesn't bleed. Don't you see?" She turned toward Curve, and he knew that her blind eyes, or whatever the hell was in there, were looking directly at him, seeing him in spite of her blindness, feeling his fear. He looked away fast. "His soul has crossed over. Ashe Corven has come back from the other side."

Oh Jesus, he *was* dead. He was really dead and came back and killed Spider Monkey and Nemo, and Curve was next. He felt as though the Crow was working its way up from his guts now, tickling his throat to make him puke in fear. He felt the first bitter taste, but swallowed it back down again. Hell, he'd *sooner* die than have a nervous barf in front of Kali.

"So," Judah said, evincing the same kind of interest he would show in a particular difficult chess puzzle, "how do you stop a man who's already dead?"

The head beneath the cowl swiveled in Judah's direction. "Can you look destiny in the eye without flinching?" Sibyl said.

Judah studied the shadows beneath the cowl. "You tell me."

This, Curve thought, was as fucking weird as all the rest of this shit. Judah was pulling a stare-down with a chick who didn't have any eyes, and that was what made it worse. Curve couldn't look at Sibyl for any time at all. She drove him absolutely apeshit, because she *knew*. She didn't have to see. She knew what was in your mind and your soul, and it was like those inner eyes of hers were just cutting through you as easy as a razor slices off an ear.

But Judah didn't falter. He just kept looking right at her until she spoke again. "The Crow is the source of his power—his link between this world and the next. Sever that link . . . and he is as vulnerable as the next man."

That seemed to be it, Curve thought. The fucking oracle had spoken, and now it was up to the rest of them to actually *do* something about it, make something practical out of Sibyl's weirdo babblings.

So what did she mean? Fill the Crow full of bullets next time he saw it? Hell, he hadn't even been able to get a bead on the big black fuck.

But when Curve looked back at Judah, he saw something cooking there. Judah had an idea, and when the main man had an idea, Curve knew the shit was heading for the fan. He just hoped that the fan would spray black feathers and blood, and that some of that blood would be Ashe Corven's.

13

CURSED CROW, WHAT ART THOU CROAKING TO
ME? THAT I SHOULD RETRACE MY STEPS?
—Aristophanes, *The Birds*

Her words haunted him. *Then you're damned.* He
would have to go back. But while he was here on this
earth again, Ashe Corven would not rest. He would
drink in every sight and sound and smell, filling up on
memories to last him . . .

For how long? Eternity? And eternity where? He
didn't know. The only thing he felt certain of was his
own abysmal ignorance. Best to put it behind now and
look at Sarah's things, find her spirit in them, and take
part of her back to . . . wherever he would go when he
was finished with his gray, cheerless work.

He sat at her vanity table, looking at the knick-
knacks and mementos gathered there. Above him hung
the ceramic black-and-white mask, the face that Sarah
had painted on his own. He looked at his face in the

mirror, then back at the mask. "What is this?" he asked her. "This mask. What does it mean?"

"It's from British theater," Sarah said. "The three faces of drama—pain, despair, and irony."

"The face is smiling on this one," Ashe said. "Is it irony, then?"

In the mirror, he saw Sarah nod. "Just because there's a smile, it doesn't mean you're happy."

Ashe remembered when he had smiled last. There had been much blood, and pain, and despair. But he had smiled. There was a difference between happiness and justice. An ironic difference? Perhaps.

At the bottom of the vanity table's mirror, Ashe saw a faded postcard tucked between the frame and the glass. He slid it free and looked at it. On the smooth finished surface, there was a carnival midway set on a beach. People strolled along a boardwalk, surrounded by golden sands and blue skies. WISH YOU WERE HERE, read the words at the top.

"I've been here," Ashe said with a touch of wonder. He stared at the picture for a long time. It fascinated him, like a magic mirror in which he could see his past. "I took Danny there last summer. We went up on the bike, rode all the way up the coast. . . ." He stared, examining every detail on the postcard, captured by wistful nostalgia for the life he had lost.

"It was cold up there," he said, remembering. "We could see each other's breath."

Ashe felt his lips start to tremble, his throat constrict. He tucked the postcard back between the frame and the mirror, and put his head down so that Sarah would not look in the mirror and see his eyes. He could feel no moisture, but thought that they must be close to brimming with tears. Desperately, he tried to think of something else, *anything* else, but everything he thought of had some connection with his past, and his past was inextricably intertwined with Danny.

He took a deep, shuddering breath, and tried to let the emotions pass, tried to ground himself in his current existence, and the mission that had created it. But then he felt her hand on his shoulder and heard her voice close to his ear.

"Look at me."

He couldn't. He sat there with his head down, refusing to meet her gaze, even in the mirror.

"Ashe," she said. "Look at me."

He turned around then, feeling that she would see only deep and lasting loss in his eyes. When he looked up at her, he had expected to see sympathy and compassion, but what he had not expected were the depths of understanding that shone from her face. It was as if she alone, among all the souls in the world, could understand the isolation that was consuming him.

He could not look away, and saw mirrored in her face the same longing that held him. Here, in this spot, at this time, there were only the two of them, with empty places in their souls that the other could fill. No one else watched or heard.

Tentatively, she leaned toward him until their faces were only inches away. She smelled like flowers, and her eyes seemed to search his soul, asking what he wanted her to do next. The moment was balanced on a knife edge, and he felt as though he would slip off at any moment.

131

And then he drew back.

"No . . ." he said, and turned away, breaking the fragile bond between them. "We can't do this. It's not why I'm here." He could not look at her. He was afraid to see in her face the hurt that he felt. "I have to finish what I started. I have to find the others."

"I know," she said, and when she took her hand from his shoulder, it was like losing a limb. Grace and mercy had fled his world, and left it to monsters.

He stood up slowly, as though he might break, and walked to the door, aching with every step, a terrible sense of longing gnawing at his heart. As he passed through the door, she called his name once, and he turned back. "I wish I'd met you before," she said.

He nodded, knowing that she knew he wished the same, then turned and left. There was nothing else to say. If he had only met her before, he thought. Before Danny had ever opened that other door, before Curve and his gang had seen them, before he had . . . died. No, there wasn't much future in loving a dead man.

The thought brought a thin smile to his face. There. That was irony, wasn't it? He was wearing the right mask after all.

He straddled his motorcycle and looked up at the front window of her loft, through which he had climbed earlier. She was there, and raised her hand as if to say good-bye, but she did not wave it. Ashe smiled, hoping that she would see the reality of it beneath the painted smile, and started the engine.

When he looked back down at the street, he saw on the other side the window of a bakery shop. Inside, there were mountains of sugar skulls, candy skeletons,

132

and *pan de muerte*, the bread of the dead. Hundreds of fleshless faces, in the brightest white accented by midnight black, stared out at him, and in the glass, his own reflection added one more black and white countenance to the morbid company. Death looking at death.

And he was death, sure and certain, to those he would visit.

He fired up the engine and raced down the street, leaving the other skeleton faces to look out at the empty night, waiting for those who would come and buy small, sweet deaths.

It moved as steadily and surely as a second hand around a clock, but not to time's purpose. The stag beetle crawled to the purpose of freedom, a freedom that would never be until the thread that bound it to its captive nail was severed.

Judah Earl easily heard the light scratching of its tiny legs, and he was sure that Sibyl could *see* the creature as it scuttled about, but he knew that he was the only person in his tower whose senses were highly developed enough to hear and enjoy its Sisyphean efforts at escape.

He heard other things as well. Curve's stomach was acting up. Judah heard the juices within it bubbling and frothing, and the occasional squeak of flatulence made him wonder why he had ever employed such a pitiful coward to be his lieutenant.

He could also hear the creak of leather and metal shifting as Kali flexed her muscles as she sat, straining one against the other, shaping her body even when seemingly still. If he concentrated very hard, he could

133

even hear the fibers of muscle moving beneath her skin. It sounded like wet rubber stretching.

But from Sibyl, he could hear nothing, nothing but her words. That was enough, if she could tell him what he needed to know.

"So the Crow is Ashe Corven's familiar," Judah said.

"Yes," Sibyl answered. "He derives his power from the bird."

"All right, then, can this power be taken, Sibyl?"

Sibyl raised her head, so that her cowl nearly fell back, but then lowered it again with a finality that told Judah she had found the answer. "The bird is the key, and the key to the bird is the life force that flows within it. . . ."

Judah understood instantly. "The blood of the Crow," he said, and then again, so softly that only Sibyl heard, "The blood of the Crow . . ."

He leaped to his feet and whirled about. He could feel his eyes blazing, could hear the blood rushing to his brain as his thoughts multiplied, his ideas coalesced. "The tattoo on your chest," he said to Curve. "Who gave it to you?"

The fool stammered for a moment, then said, "Uh, some bitch down at the Gargoyle."

"The *what*?"

"The Gray Gargoyle—it's a tattoo shop. But what's that got to do with—"

Judah grasped Curve's shoulders and shook him, and the man's mouth snapped shut. Judah could smell his fear. "It's got *everything* to do with it, you idiot!

Find her! Right now! If she gave you the mark of the Crow, then she's connected to him in some way.

"She can lead us to him!"

He hurled Curve toward the door. Curve stumbled, but caught himself, and ran out, not looking back. Kali followed, walking boldly and without fear. It might seem ironic to some, Judah thought, that his finest warrior was a woman. But to him it was logical. If his greatest adviser was female, why not then his strongest arm? Things would be much more pleasant, though, if Kali hadn't wanted to kill him. But then, Kali wanted to kill everyone.

He turned back to the figure sitting in the shadows. "Thank you, Sibyl," he said graciously. "You give me the clues, I weave together the tapestry. Find the woman, find the Crow, find Ashe Corven. And his power. Imagine, all the power that the Crow, the avatar of death, can grant." Judah shook his head at the magnitude of it. "Ashe Corven must be a very happy man indeed."

The waters looked thick and viscous. He could taste them in his mind, remembering how they had flowed over his tongue, into his nostrils, down his throat, and into his stomach and his lungs. He remembered how those waters had blazed in his chest, tightening his muscles, locking their fire inside until it burned his life away, and his blood mingled with the water, drifting up as he sank farther and farther down, bound to his son in life and death.

Ashe Corven looked away from the waters at the end of the pier where he and Danny had met their deaths, and focused his eyes on the wood instead. The stain was still there. Danny's blood had soaked into the boards, and the sin of that crime would remain for a long time. He looked for the stain his blood had made, and found it easily.

It made sense that it was larger than Danny's. A man was far bigger than a child, and would have more blood in him, wouldn't he? Of course he would.

Ashe gave a sharp, bitter laugh. Of such musings was madness made. Amounts of blood, weights of bodies, temperature required to reduce to ash, liters of gas needed per hundred subjects. Butchery, genocide, the death of children. See evil and die, no questions asked or answered, no mercy shown but the mercy of the gas, the fallout, the bullet. Oh, what an angelic place was this City of Angels. Deadly new world, that hath such monsters in it!

He clutched his head in his hands to drive out the mad thoughts. He had work to do, and had come here to remember, all too vividly, why. Danny's picture pressed against his chest like a finger prodding him to action, and he took it out and unfolded it, looked again at the man and the boy and the names DAD and ME.

It was different now, he thought dully, and realized why. It had bullet holes in it from the bullets that had been shot at him and failed to harm him. The same kind of bullets that had killed him, and had killed Danny.

He laughed and cried as he wondered, Why now? Why *now* could the bullets fail to harm him? Why could he and Danny have not been blessed with such power when they needed it, before this had all started?

What gods made these decisions? And how in heaven or hell did they choose their timing? Then a blessing, now a curse, death and life, both unsought, but *forced* upon you at the whim of what crazed deity, or what fickle, insane fate!

Ashe Corven raised his face to the skies and screamed, cursing his blessing, living his death, dying inside, in the midst of unwanted life.

14

CROW-BILL: A FORCEPS FOR EXTRACTING BULLETS
OR OTHER FOREIGN BODIES FROM
WOUNDS.

—*Oxford English Dictionary*

While Ashe Corven screamed from the depths of his soul, Noah would have given his soul to be able to scream. The tattoo artist had been duct-taped to the dentist chair in the Gray Gargoyle. Even his mouth and nose had been sealed shut so that he could not breathe.

Today was November 1, la Noche de los Muertos, and he and Sarah had decided to keep the shop closed in the afternoon and open it after dark. Daylight business had been slow anyway, and Sarah had been acting so bloody strange in the past day or two that Noah figured she could stand a bit of a rest.

Hell, so could he, for that matter. Maybe it was being around her that was a downer, or maybe it was the whole Days of the Dead routine, but he felt pretty shagged himself. He'd slept through most of the day, and then hauled himself down to the shop just after dark.

The streets had been nearly empty. The celebration wouldn't start in earnest until midnight, and most of the celebrants were taking it easy until then. Noah had thought that he and Sarah would get a raft of clients once the party started. Many people required a little booze in their systems before they would come in a tattoo parlor and ask for tattoos of skulls and angels and other intimations of mortality and immortality. La Noche de los Muertos was one helluva business night for ink pushers.

In fact, he had first thought that his captors were after tattoos. The bird looked the type anyway as she climbed out of her car, all metal and leather and attitude. A little meaner than he liked, maybe, but it would have made a pleasant evening running a needle over her skin.

But when the dude who pulled in next to her got off his motorcycle, and Noah saw who it was, he tried to lock the door. The woman was too fast, and had kicked it in before he could secure it in its new frame. Two huge men, identical as far as Noah could see, climbed out of her car and barreled in after her, and then came the one called Curve, who had already stuck a gun in Noah's face and nearly killed him.

The two men had grabbed Noah, one from either side, and he might just as well have tried to shake off a pair of gorillas. They held him down in the chair, while the woman and Curve secured him to it, wrapping that sodding duct tape all around him, and then

140

the blond gorillas went outside, probably to keep anyone else from coming into the shop.

"What the fuck is this?" Noah demanded, but before he could get out another word, the woman had wrapped the heavy gray tape around his mouth. He tried to make sounds through his improvised gag, but then terror iced his brain as the woman ripped off another hunk of tape and pressed it over his nose tightly, closing his nostrils so that he couldn't breathe at all.

Blood rushed to his head, and he thrashed about savagely, as though that would somehow loosen the tape. It didn't, and he felt as though his eyes were popping out of their sockets, and his head was getting ready to explode.

Curve reached for his face, but the woman, who had been watching his struggle mercilessly, stopped him. "Goddamnit, Kali," Curve said, "he can't tell us nothin' if he's dead."

"He won't die for several minutes," Noah heard the woman say over the sound of rushing water in his ears.

The pain and the panic increased, and soon he could see nothing at all. He felt himself sliding down into darkness, when pain flared on his face, and he was able to breathe again. The tape ripping off his skin had taken away what little breath he had left, but now he gasped in sweet air so frenziedly that it made him cough.

He hacked for nearly a minute. Then his vision cleared, and he looked up at his tormentors. "What do you want?" he said weakly. "What the bloody hell do you people *want*?"

"A house in the country," Curve said, sarcasm edging his voice. "A dog, a wife, and two kids . . ." When he grinned, there was not a trace of humor in it. "Your fucking head stapled to my saddlebags."

"We're looking for Sarah," the woman called Kali said. "Where is she, Noah?"

"I don't know, luv."

"Of course you do. You've worked with her, you're friends, you certainly know where she lives. Where is she, Noah?"

He wondered what to do. He couldn't tell them where Sarah was. They were crazy. They probably wanted to kill her because of the other night, when she had held Curve's own gun on him and chased him from the shop. He had *told* her that she would be sorry she hadn't killed him, and right now Noah sure as shit was.

But what the hell to do? If he told them, they'd probably kill him anyway, especially if they intended to do Sarah. Then he realized that he was dead. They would kill him either way. So if he was already a dead man, he didn't have to tell them crap.

He gave up on himself then, and said, with more calm than he had thought himself capable of, "I'm not goin' to tell you where she is, luv."

Kali shook her head almost sadly, as though she disliked what she was going to have to do now. "Oh, but I think you are," she said, and then spread her legs and straddled the bottom of the dentist chair, moving up over his feet and legs until she sat astride his hips. Then she lowered her weight onto him, and he felt her warmth against his groin, and was aroused in spite of himself.

Was this how the crazy bitch was planning to get in-formation, by lap-dancing him into submission? Fat fucking chance. But then Kali reached out lazily for one of the tattoo machines. When the needle was in her hand, she nodded to Curve, who hit the treadle switch that turned on the rapidly whirring needle. Noah's erection vanished, and he eyed with deep fear the sparking tattoo machine that Kali was slowly moving toward his face.

Closer and closer it came, until the whining needle was a vibrating blur only centimeters from Noah's blinking right eye. Finally he couldn't stand it anymore and pressed his eyes shut. But then he felt Kali's thumb cruelly pressing upward on his right eyelid, and he was forced to watch as the needle came ever closer.

"Last chance, 'luv,' " Kali said.

He was dead, oh bleedin' Christ, he was dead, and they were going to make him hurt first. Well, fuck 'em, if they did they did, and there wasn't a damn thing he could do about it, except not tell them what they wanted to know. Yeah. Fuck 'em. Maybe he could piss them off enough to make them kill him fast.

Noah gathered as much spittle as he could in his dry mouth, and said, "Get *bent,* you dried-up bitch!" Then he spat the gob full into Kali's face.

When the limey kid screamed, Curve knew Kali had lost it. And when he saw the blood spraying up over her shoulder, he knew that they weren't going to get anything more out of the Brit.

"Aw *shit,* Kali!" Curve said, coming around to where he could see exactly what was going down. The

143

needle was, to be specific. Right down through the kid's eye socket and into his skull. The sight made Curve purse his lips, but he didn't look away. He had seen worse. "Oh yeah," he said sarcastically. "He's gonna tell us a *whole* fuckin' lot now."

Kali pulled back her hand and wiped the blood on the dead kid's shirt. "He dishonored me," she said, and her voice was as shaky as Curve had ever heard it.

"Yeah?" he said, going after the weakness. "What'd he do, Kali, press a stiff one against your crotch?" Then he saw the spittle glistening on her face, along with Noah's blood, and gave a laugh, but just a little one. This was one pissed-off female assassin here. "It wipes off, babe. Same as blood."

Kali yanked a silk handkerchief from a fold in her clothing and passed it over her face again and again, until only a few traces of smeared blood remained. "They probably have a john in here," he said. "With running water?"

Without a word, Kali dismounted from her victim and went into the back of the shop. Curve started opening desk drawers. By the time Kali had come back, he had found some business papers with Sarah's name and home address on them. He looked up at Kali, whose face was now washed clean. There was a benefit to leather and metal, Curve thought. Blood wiped off damn easy.

He held up the papers. "Bingo," he said. "The little bitch's address. Let's book."

As they walked out of the shop, Curve suddenly stopped, wincing. His chest hurt, not deep like a heart attack might feel, but as though someone were scratching at his flesh with claws. He opened his light coat and looked down at his chest.

The tattoo of the crow was dripping blood from its beak and talons, blood that was trickling slowly down Curve's chest and over his belly.

Curve put his hand to his chest, looked at the blood on his fingers, and staggered back. But he could not escape what was happening to his own flesh. "No . . . no . . ." he said, looking down with horror at his blood oozing from the tattoo.

"What is it?" Kali asked clinically, but Curve wasn't listening. He yanked his jacket closed, as if shutting up a dirty secret in a closet, and ran to his bike, climbed on, and hit the ignition.

"Curve!" Kali shouted after him, but he was long gone.

At first Curve didn't know where to go or what to do. The goddamn Crow and that Corven guy could be anywhere. But then he thought that he would be safer in a place where a lot of his crew were, so he swerved around a corner and headed for the Second Coming fetish club.

As he drove, he constantly looked behind him, and to the sides. He also looked up. Where the Crow was, maybe Ashe Corven would be too. But he didn't see the big black motherfucker, and there wasn't anybody who looked like Corven among the faces he passed in the street.

The Second Coming's oceans of flesh had always seemed comforting to him before, like a hot, sweaty womb that sheltered and stimulated him at the same time. But tonight the writhing, intertwined carpet of aroused bodies was nightmarish, and there was nowhere to escape.

La Noche de los Muertos seemed to be making everyone prove that they were alive, and the best way to do that was by fucking and sucking and toking and snorting. The celebration had even moved into the usually sedate bar. The naked flesh of the celebrants looked dead and pale under the dim lights, and the air seemed thick and cloying, reeking of cheap perfume unsuccessfully masking rank sweat and the odor of corpses.

Curve pushed his way through the heaving, bucking mass of bodies to the bar, fell onto a stool, and dug out another glassine bag of Trinity. He ripped it open and vacuum snorted it, throwing back his head and closing his eyes.

Let it happen, damn it!

And it did. It hit him with its full, blessed force, and for a few moments, at any rate, he was free of fear and pain as the chemicals flowed. But then, like a killer waiting just around the corner, the pain came back, tearing through his body, and he dropped the envelope and fell against the bar, his hands clawing at his chest again, feeling the blood soaking through his jacket.

". . . goawaygoawaygoawaygoaway . . ." he moaned. But the pain didn't go away, and he knew that the killer who had been waiting had finally arrived.

The music seemed to fade, swallowed up by the foul air until all that remained was the sound of drums, muted and far, as though calling warriors to battle.

Their song was doom, and doom, heavy and inexorable, settled over Curve's heart and mind.

The time had come, and he lifted his head, although it felt so very heavy, and looked at himself in the mirror over the bar, past the longneck the Samoan bartender had set in front of him, past the rows of bottles, through the haze of smoke and sweat.

His face looked like a dead man's. And he thought that he could see, materializing like a ghost just above his dying face, the Angel of Death waiting for him. Yes, there he was, his face painted white, a black smile curving his lips, dressed all in black, the color of death, striding through the narcotic haze, wading through the sea of bodies toward Curve. The others saw, they knew who he was, and their hands came away from bare breasts, out of wet crevices, from around cylinders of flesh, and reached toward him as though touching him would grant them some portion of his majesty.

The Angel's hand came up as if in blessing, but then Curve saw what that hand held, and realized with a shattering clarity that this was no angel.

Angels didn't carry sawed-offs.

The black eye of the barrel stared at Curve, and he dived for the floor as it spat a fistful of shot over his head, shattering the bar mirror and a score of bottles. Bourbon and scotch and gin and tequila and a dozen other liquors were mixed in a massive airborne cocktail garnished with glass that showered over Curve.

He staggered to his feet and started running, pushing through the press of panicked, half-clothed and naked bodies. When he looked back, the sight literally froze him with terror.

The fat Samoan bartender had tried to come to Curve's—and the bar's—rescue. He was opening up on Ashe Corven with a semiauto pistol, spraying bullets at the man with total disregard for bystanders, and Curve saw a couple of prime pieces of flesh explode in red wetness. Three of the Second Coming's bodyguards were firing at Corven too, with big, nasty, fucking guns that spat out fire along with their bullets. They caught their share of innocents too, if the patrons of the Second Coming could be considered innocent.

But it wasn't the rain of bullets or the falling orgiasts that shocked Curve. Instead it was the fact that Ashe Corven was being hit by a good ninety percent of the bullets thrown, and the son-of-a-bitch was *still coming*.

The guy was a fucking human candle. Bullets were exploding all over his body, tearing his black leather duster to shreds, but they didn't do a damn thing to stop him. Slow him down, maybe, but he shook off their effect like they were gnats instead of a hail of high-caliber gunfire.

Finally the Samoan and the bodyguards stopped firing and just looked at their target. Corven kept walking toward them, smoking holes riddling his leather clothing. The bodyguards broke and ran. At last, when Corven was only several feet away, Curve heard the Samoan mutter, "Aw, fuck this," and turn tail.

"Just you and me, pal," Ashe Corven said, pausing for a moment as if he was savoring the situation.

The pause gave Curve the chance he needed to come to his senses, and he ran like a bat out of hell, filled with the energy only the fear of death can bring. His booted feet pounded on and over bodies, living, dead, and wounded, clattering through doorways, down stairs and dingy halls until he reached the back door.

He stormed through it, taking the stairs to the street three and four at a time, spilling into a couple of back-alley junkies, who howled indignantly after him. He stumbled into a pile of garbage, scattered some rats, and finally reached his bike. The key took forever to find, and flop sweat claimed him when he thought he had lost it. But it was there, and he shoved it into the ignition and hit the starter switch. . . .

And Ashe Corven came flying off the second floor fire escape like the Crow that gave him his strength. He landed on the roof of a car right next to Curve, and the impact made the windows pop, spraying Curve with bits of safety glass.

Corven squatted there on all fours, like a wolf about to pounce, glaring down at Curve. "Time's up, Curve," he said, but did not move.

"Fuck you, bird-dick!" Curve shouted, and jerked his bike toward the street and gunned it, thinking, Bird-dick? Even with death on his tail, Curve despaired at not being able to find *le mot juste*. Bird-dick? Jesus, he thought, I *must* be fucking scared. . . .

But his fear began to fade as he heard no one in pursuit, and that damn tattoo on his chest hadn't been aching for a while. Curve felt almost reborn as he raced through the streets, looking into the store windows he shot past to catch a glimpse of himself, alive and alone, roaring through the night.

Then he made the mistake of glancing behind him. Ashe Corven was not pursuing him, but the Crow was nearly at his shoulder.

He shrieked, the terror back like an addiction, and turned into an alley, his tachometer red-lining. He shot out onto another street, swung around, and headed for the labyrinth of streets and alleys down by the river.

He looked back and saw nothing. But just as he was about to congratulate himself, the Crow plunged down at him from out of the night sky, its wings flapping madly, gaining on Curve like the breath of Death.

Curve drove. He had no idea where he was going. The only thought in his mind was *escape,* and it chimed like a great bell. He knew the City of Angels well, all its mean streets and dirty alleys. Now he raced by a warehouse, leaning in low, trying to urge on his bike by sheer will.

Past the warehouse, he veered off the road onto railroad tracks, and rattled down them. He swept around industrial chimneys, swerved around billboards, ducked under laundry lines that might have decapitated him had he been less alert. Then, finally, back on a deserted street.

Above the roar of his engine, Curve could hear another sound, an unmuffled growl, and he knew that there was another bike somewhere near. He looked back, but saw nothing, not even the Crow. Nothing to the sides, or ahead of him. Then he looked up.

Thirty feet above, on a highway overpass paralleling the street Curve was on, rode Ashe Corven. The black bird was flying at Corven's shoulder, and as Curve watched, his attention suicidally away from the road he traveled, the Crow landed on Corven's shoulder and rode there. Despite the speed of Corven's bike, its feathers were unruffled. It sat steadily, not even leaning into the wind, like a ghost in some other dimension, unaffected by the things of this world.

Curve looked back at the street just in time to see a late-night delivery van rolling into the street. He grasped his handlebars and swerved around it, then hit the throttle again. Fuck him, he told himself. He knew there was no way off the overpass for two miles, and by then there would be plenty of side streets down which Curve could vanish into the night.

At the side of the overpass up ahead, Curve saw a gaping break in the guardrail. Fucking city, he thought. Have to have some family go through that bastard before they'd get it fixed. For a brief second the thought of the break made Curve uneasy, until he told himself to forget it, no fucking way. Then he was past it, and from high above he heard the high-pitched whine of wheels spinning with no traction beneath them.

He looked back and up, and saw Ashe Corven falling through the air down toward the street, saw the Crow leave the man's shoulder and rise up to the sky. The crazy asshole had jumped into thin air through the gap in the guardrail.

Curve saw him hit, saw the tires bounce him into the air again, saw him come down just ten yards behind Curve. Nobody could have done that, thought Curve. Nobody human.

The engine of Curve's bike screamed as he rode it full throttle. He would be all right, he told himself, trying to believe it. His bike was just as powerful as Corven's, and he had been riding ever since his legs had been long enough to touch the ground. As long as there was an open street, he could stay ahead of Corven, and maybe get away.

But if not, how long could he ride? Not forever, and he was afraid that riding forever was exactly what Ashe Corven could do.

MY WINE OF LIFE IS POISON MIXED WITH GALL.
—James Thomson, "The City of Dreadful Night"

Forever.

Sarah looked again at the word engraved on the inside of the ring before she let it fall back on its chain against her neck. Then she looked at the painting again.

Forever was what she wanted in the work, but it wasn't quite there yet. The woman, the man, the dark people hovering about the bedside, all of it bespoke finality and completion, but with an ending, not a going-on. She had not yet captured *Forever.*

Gabriel, sleeping on a small throw rug, suddenly woke and leaped to his feet. He looked up toward the ceiling, hissing.

Sarah looked up automatically, hoping to see Ashe at the skylight, but instead the Crow stood on the glass, its head bent to look down at them, feet splayed on the smooth surface. It watched her and did not move, and Sarah watched it in turn, until a knock at the door distracted her.

She ran to it, thinking that if the Crow had returned, so had Ashe. But long habit kept her from opening the many locks and flinging back the door at once, and she peered through the keyhole to see who stood on the other side while she said, "Who is it?"

Sarah saw the fish-eye image of a woman she did not know. She was clad like a metal rocker and cradled a nasty-looking automatic weapon in her arms. On either side of her were two identical, beefy, blond-haired twin men. "Open it up," the woman said, in a voice that Sarah thought sounded like a man's.

Sarah backed away from the door, looking for a way out, but there was only the window, and she knew she could not climb down from there. It was a moot point anyway, for the woman on the other side of the door said, "Suit yourself. Stand back or get shot."

Sarah didn't hesitate. She grabbed Gabriel and ran into the bathroom as the shots began. The locks held, but the door didn't. The bullets weakened the frame until the three outside were able to start breaking it down. Only then did Sarah remember the pistol of Curve's that she had stuck in one of the kitchen drawers. But it was too late now.

From the bathroom, she listened to the sound of cracking wood, and shoved Gabriel inside a closet, pushing it shut, hoping they wouldn't find her cat, that at least he would be all right.

She heard the door splinter apart and the footsteps

cross the loft to the bathroom. The door was yanked open, and the woman looked in at her contemptuously. "You have someplace to go," the woman said, "and someone to meet."

Kali reached in and grabbed the woman around the neck, training the muzzle of the weapon on her face. Some would have called that face beautiful, but Kali thought it too refined and delicate. It was the kind of face into which she would have enjoyed pumping a bullet.

But the girl was not to be harmed. Those were Judah Earl's orders, and Kali would follow them for now, until the moment came when she could take over Judah Earl's kingdom for herself. It would be difficult, but it would happen, if she only retained her discipline.

That hollow-eyed sow, Sibyl, was the sticking point. While Judah would have willingly believed that all his deputies were loyal and as loving as those who kill for a living can be, Sibyl could read their hearts and tell Judah what she saw there. So it was that Curve, that trembling coward, was given access to the lord and master anytime. He didn't have the balls to kill Judah and then take over, and Judah knew it.

But Kali was not so honored. Kali was dangerous. Indeed, she prided herself on being the most dangerous of them all, and the most ruthless. None of the others would have shot the little boy the other night, but Kali had not hesitated. And she had felt nothing, either, nothing except the joy of seeing another enemy die. It had always been so, ever since she had killed for the first time, when she was fourteen.

She had never had reason to be angry as a child. Her parents were wealthy, and were both good to her, giving her everything she wanted, within reason. The one thing they had not given her, and which Kali, goddess of death, demanded, was lives.

It had begun so simply. She was standing with her younger brother on a high bluff one summer day, when their family had gone on a picnic. They were both looking down at the ocean, staying back several feet from the edge, when she looked around and realized that no one else was in sight.

There was not even any thought involved, only her need. She wanted to push him from the bluff, and that want, combined with the fact that there was no one to see, propelled her forward. She shoved him hard, and he stumbled toward the edge, then over, screaming as he went down. She watched his descent over the rough rocks, his body bouncing down toward the sea, leaving a trail of blood until it struck the water, and his arms and legs danced in the waves.

Her heart danced too, and she knew that the death of others was the purpose of her life. Then she ran back to where her parents were, weeping with joy that they saw as horror.

After that, she could not remain in her home, with her family. She must have death, and if she remained, death would have them. She would have reveled in their deaths, as she would have reveled in any death. But their deaths would have cast suspicion on her, and there were so many lives unconnected to her own that it was foolish to pluck grapes from her own vineyard.

She left her home and went to the City of Angels,

where she had heard lives were cheap. She took lives as soon as she arrived, and stole the money from the corpses of those she killed. With that money, she paid for the services of those who knew and would teach her the ways of death.

When she began her training, she was already proficient in the use of firearms. By her seventeenth year, she knew over a hundred methods to kill with her hands and feet. By her nineteenth, she had added to her repertoire all the weapons of the Orient.

When she turned twenty-one, she had used all those methods and all those weapons, and had earned the name of Kali. She kept herself pure, using no drugs or alcohol or tobacco. She had never once had sex, nor had she ever desired it. Nothing a man could do could touch the feelings that possessed her when she killed. Blood was the only thing to which she was addicted.

It was only natural that she would eventually attract the attention of Judah Earl, and when she considered the benefits of working for him—protection from arrest, wealth, and best of all, an unending source of lives to take—she agreed to do his killing for him. It was a bountiful harvest.

But she wanted what he had in the City of Angels, the ultimate power over life and death, and it would one day be hers. Until that glorious day, she trained and disciplined herself, and she killed and she waited and did Judah's bidding.

And his will was that this woman Sarah should be brought to him unharmed. She would be. But Kali first wanted to see pain in her limpid eyes.

She pushed Sarah out of the bathroom and into the

157

main room of the loft, then threw her down on the couch and pressed the muzzle of the gun against her head. "You move or even speak, and you will die," she told her. Then she spoke to the twins, the two walking piles of muscle who did what she said the way she did what Judah said. "Destroy this place. Break everything."

They did, and the woman sat there trembling but silent as she watched her world being torn apart. The pain was there in her eyes, and it was good, but not as good as her death would have been. Still, it was a start.

16

AND WHAT DOES THE CROW SAY ABOUT THE ROAD
TO FOLLOW?

—Aristophanes, *The Birds*

There was a bridge ahead that would take them out of
the City of Angels. Curve was approaching it at well
past ninety. But instead of shooting across it, he
swerved at the last minute, cutting down a roadway
that ran by the river, praying to God and the devil that
Ashe Corven wouldn't see him.

He had been able to outdistance the dead man, and
hoped that Corven would just drive on across the
bridge and keep going forever. And even if he followed him, maybe Curve could still hole up in this
place he knew about.

At the bottom of the road, there was a tunnel spillway, with a chain-link fence running across its mouth.
The shadow of a big tree hid a hole in the fence from
the light of a single street lamp, and Curve pulled his

bike off the road, aiming it into that welcoming darkness. Then he sped into the dark tunnel, splashing through puddles of water, whipping past graffiti and empty beer cans.

As he neared the dim light at the other end of the tunnel, he slowed, knowing that the tunnel sloped sharply downward to the concrete riverbed. He cut his engine and sat in the darkness, waiting, hoping for the silence that would tell him that Ashe Corven had gone past, and he had lost him.

Curve sat straddling his bike, listening to the sounds of night. Insects called, far away a siren howled, and in the tunnel the water drip-drip-dripped all around him. He could feel it creeping into his boots, but he dared not move, not yet, not for another few minutes. And then he could go back to Judah's.

That was it. He would ask Judah what to do. He felt like kicking himself. He had been so fucking panicked that he hadn't even thought of that. If anyone would know how to finish this zombie motherfucker, it was Judah.

But then he heard the motorcycle. Corven's bike. It wasn't loud. It was moving slow, as though it were a horse that Corven was riding, hunting his prey in thick brush. Curve watched the other end of the tunnel. He felt as though his tongue was growing bigger and bigger, soaking up all the spit, so that his mouth felt dry as dust.

Corven's bike engine slowed even more, and finally stopped. At the far end of the tunnel, where Curve had entered, a silhouette stepped into his view. It was Corven, clutching something in his hand that Curve knew could only be the sawed-off shotgun.

160

The sound of his engine didn't matter now. Curve started his bike and backed it up to the edge of the tunnel, intending to swing it around and shoot down the slope, coming out on the edge of the riverbed, down which he would escape. But when he took his eyes off his pursuer long enough to look down the slope of the spillway, he saw that there was no edge at all. The waters were high and rushing, all the way to the edge of the concrete, and the walls were so high that he could not get over them.

Shit! Sweet fucking shit! He remembered too late that there had been a long dry spell when he had capped a squealer here last summer. And the past few weeks had seen some of the heaviest rains in the City of Angels before it finally stopped. There would be no escape.

It was as if Corven had read Curve's mind. A mad laugh rang down the tunnel, chilling Curve to the bone. Then Corven spoke, and the words echoed around the concrete:

" 'I have a rendezvous with Death,
    On some scarred slope of battered hill. . . .' "

Ashe Corven started walking down the tunnel toward Curve. His wet footsteps echoed like his words off the weeping walls.

" 'God knows 'twere better to be deep
    Where love throbs out in blissful sleep,
    Pulse nigh to pulse and breath to breath. . . .' "

Now the man's deathlike face emerged from the gloom, a ghastly visage floating in the ether, lit by the lights bouncing off the river below.

"'But I have a rendezvous with Death.
And I to my pledged word am true—'"

He stopped twenty feet away from Curve, grinning like some crazed Cheshire cat. Curve felt piss start to wet his pants as Ashe Corven softly finished his poem:

"'I shall not fail that rendezvous.'"

The silence hung like knives in the tunnel. He heard only the drip of the water from above, a steady drip-drip-drip that seemed to mock Curve's fear even more than Corven's grin. Then Curve realized what he had done.

Piss. He had pissed his fucking pants. He had never done that before, never. Who the hell was this crazy fuck anyway, to make him piss his pants?

The thought infuriated Curve, and he shrieked at the man. "You think I'm afraid of you, you fucking *freak*? *You think I'm afraid?*"

A scream of pure animal rage ripped from Curve's throat, and he gunned his cycle forward, rolling the throttle all the way open in a kamikaze run aimed straight at Ashe Corven. He saw the crazy painted bastard stand his ground and raise his shotgun, and Curve thought: *Fine, you fuck, let's both die then. . . .*

Ashe Corven fired the shotgun directly at the customized painting of the woman fucking Death on the teardrop gas tank. Their orgasm shook Curve's world.

The motorcycle disintegrated beneath him, turning into a cloud of flaming shrapnel that bled him and slashed him and pierced him. He and the bike were suddenly a rushing comet of flaming wreckage that skidded along the tunnel walls, and as the flames seared his eyes, Curve saw that the rocket of destruction he and the metal had become was still heading straight toward Corven. Then everything went red and black at once.

When Curve could think again, he knew he was lying on the tunnel floor in mud and garbage and puddles of his own blood and burning gasoline. He raised his head and opened his eyes.

The first thing he saw was a barb of steel sticking up from his chest. Right through that fucking crow tattoo, he thought. And then he looked where Ashe Corven had been standing, where the fire burned as high and hot as the flames of hell, and Curve laughed in a moment of giddy, glorious victory. I may have bought it, but I got you, you freak.

Then Ashe Corven stepped out of the flames as calmly as if he were walking through a spring breeze, and Curve's charred jaw dropped in amazement. Corven stopped directly in front of him and looked down. He was not grinning now. "Can you hear me, Curve?"

Curve gave a weak nod.

"You're going to die now."

He tried to say something, but felt blood spill from

163

his mouth. There was a lot of it, and he coughed so it would not choke him.

Ashe Corven put a finger to his lips, telling Curve to be quiet. All right, Curve thought. Whatever you want. There was no fight left in him. He felt like a baby, a baby that had pissed itself and needed to be changed. And he would be. More than his pants would be changed. Oh yes, there was a big change coming on soon.

Corven dropped down next to him, kneeling over Curve's chest. He reached beneath Curve's coat and took the .45 from his holster. "This can't be comfortable," he said, and made the gun disappear into his own coat.

Then Corven looked into his eyes. "People used to put coins in the mouths of the dead," he said. "Do you know why?"

Yes, he was a child now, and Ashe was telling him a story. He made a little noise in his throat to say no, he didn't know why.

"So they could pay the ferryman to take them across the River Styx." Ashe reached to the side of Curve's head, where he couldn't see what he was doing. "What's this?" Ashe said.

A magic trick. Ashe had taken something from out of Curve's ear, wasn't that amazing? And now he held it in front of Curve's eyes. A coin. Curve almost smiled. Ashe flipped the coin back and forth, and a golden eye opened and closed, winking at Curve. Curve thought it was a good trick.

"Open your mouth, Curve."

Oh no. That frightened Curve. Only bad people had

ever told him to open his mouth, like that dentist the time his teeth were all bad, and the men who gave his mother money so that she would let them do things to him. *Open your mouth, kid.* He remembered what had happened, and he moaned.

"Shh . . ." Ashe whispered. "It's the coin for the Styx. You want to get across, don't you? It's not so bad. Trust me. I've been there."

He believed Ashe, and he slowly opened his mouth. Tears ran from his eyes at the memories, but he trusted Ashe, he *did*. The coin felt cool on his tongue, and then he remembered the single time he had gone into a church and taken the wafer on his tongue.

Ashe stood up, and Curve felt him grab the collar of his jacket, felt Ashe drag him toward the end of the tunnel that sloped down to the water. Ashe went around the puddles of fire, and Curve was glad he did. Then they went down the slope to the river, the Styx. That was where he would get on the ferry, wasn't it?

At the water's edge, Curve listened to the waves slapping against the concrete. It sounded cool and warm at the same time. He felt his body enter the water, felt it close around him. The rocking felt good. Ashe still held him so that he would not float away. "I want to thank you for showing me my pain, Curve," Ashe said. "You made me what I am."

Curve wanted to tell Ashe that he was welcome, that he was glad to help Ashe, but he had no words left. He hoped Ashe knew how he felt too, that it was all right now, that he was rocking in the arms of a mother who loved him, and was carrying him away to somewhere better than he had ever been, to be someone better than he was.

His arms outstretched, Curve floated away, down the river, shadows falling fast over his shadowed mind as his long hair fanned out upon the water. The last thing he saw were the faces staring down at him as he floated beneath a bridge. They were vagrants who had made their home in the bridge's wide underbelly, but Curve saw angels in heaven, and his eyes closed in the cloud of marigold petals one of the women let drift down upon him, and they did not open again.

The petals clustered around his body in the shape of a large crow. He remained in the center, above the place where the bird's heart would have been.

Curve, at rest, continued to float downstream toward an estuary, borne away on the wings of the Crow.

Ashe watched him go. He had felt Curve's pain and fear, and knew that they had been inside him for a very long time. That did not dismiss what Curve had become or excuse what he had done, but it helped Ashe to understand.

He turned away and walked back up the tunnel. Halfway through, he stopped at the place where Curve had fallen, and knelt down, lowering his head. He grieved for Curve, for Danny, and for himself, and wished that things could be different from the way they were, even as he was certain that they could not be.

Then he stood, determined to see his mission through to its end. It was time. Judah. Kali . . .

And there she was—in front of his eyes, or the

Crow's eyes, for he knew he saw what the bird saw. There was Sarah, and Kali pointing a gun at her, two men grabbing roughly at her arms . . . and then he was back in the tunnel, the seeping concrete surrounding him.

"Sarah!" he cried, running toward his bike. She was in trouble, but where? He leaped on the motorcycle and raced up the roadway, away from the bridge, back to the cruel streets of the City of Angels.

He skidded around corners, scattering the celebrants who were gathering in the streets, until he came to the Gray Gargoyle. The lights were off, but the door yielded to his push, and he turned on the overhead light just inside.

Noah was dead, bound to the dentist chair. There was nothing that Ashe could do to help him. Several drawers and the filing cabinet had been rifled, the papers in them scattered about. He knew what had happened, and ran out to the street, started his bike, and laid a patch of rubber directly toward Sarah's loft.

He pounded up the steps of her building and through the open door. She wasn't there, and the loft had been thoroughly trashed. It had not been done to find something, but out of pure anger. Paintings were slashed, furniture was turned over and broken.

The ceramic mask of irony was smashed into a dozen pieces.

"Sarah!" Ashe cried, looking for her behind the furniture, under the piles of ruined canvases.

"Sarah's gone, ghost man."

ORPHANS FOR THEIR PARENTS' TIMELESS DEATH
SHALL RUE THE HOUR THAT EVER THOU WAST
  BORN.
THE OWL SHRIEK'D AT THY BIRTH, AN EVIL SIGN;
THE NIGHT-CROW CRIED, ABODING LUCKLESS
  TIME. . . .

—Shakespeare, *Henry VI, Part 3*

If Kali had not disciplined herself so intensely, she would have smiled at the look of surprise on Ashe Corven's face as he whirled around. But she didn't. Her features maintained the stolidity they had been trained to achieve. She was an idol of hard stone on which this man would be broken, his life sacrificed.

The twins had taken Sarah to Judah Earl, but Kali had remained behind. She had thought Ashe Corven would come here first, looking for the girl, and she was right. She wanted it this way, just her and Corven.

If what Curve had said was true, then Corven was a walking dead man. Kali had never killed the dead before, but there was a first time for everything. She wondered what his death would taste like, and seeing

169

him standing before her like a dark ghost, she knew it would be glorious.

She breathed silently and deeply through her flared nostrils, preparing for another death, another worshiper.

.

At the first sight of her, Ashe knew the woman standing like a statue in the shadows. It was Kali, whom he had not seen since the night she had killed his son. But vengeance was not the first thing that came to his mind. "Where is she?" he demanded.

She stepped from behind a stack of Sarah's paintings, and Ashe saw that she was dressed for war. There was a katana secured in a black scabbard, twin daggers on each hip, and a bandolier of throwing darts over her chest. "She's in Judah Earl's tower. He's waiting for you there."

"You took my son's life," Ashe said. Now that he knew Sarah was alive, he remembered that he had a debt to pay.

The woman was like stone, or maybe, Ashe thought, ice was more accurate. She seemed incapable of any emotion that did not require detachment. She had probably slaughtered Danny with as little thought as swatting a fly. Her next words reinforced his impression. "Some people are born victims."

Ashe shook his head. "It takes two to make a murder."

Kali unsheathed her katana. It slid from the scabbard with the sound of demons whispering. The edge of the blade caught the glare of the streetlight outside the window, and winked at Ashe, promising death and destruction. He moved away from her, toward the half-moon window, and she slowly moved to the other side of the loft so that the wide floor separated them.

He had no doubt that her katana was sharp enough to sever muscle and bone with one swing, and wondered if his powers of regeneration were strong enough to reattach a missing limb, or even his head. It was a picture he didn't like thinking about.

But he didn't have to any longer. Kali was ready to fight. "If it takes two," she said, "then shall we dance?"

He would end it quickly. Sarah was in Judah Earl's hands, so there was no time to waste.

Kali came at him blindingly fast across the wide loft, spinning and cartwheeling end over end like something out of a Hong Kong action movie, and arrived in front of him with a deft somersault. As her feet slapped the floor for the final time, her blade became a whirling blur, rushing wings and unseen fangs snapping at Ashe's neck.

It was all over fast. Ashe ducked under the blade and came up close, using both hands to trap Kali's sword arm near her shoulder. He twisted once, hard, and heard her arm snap.

Before she had a chance to cry out, he pivoted, throwing her over his hip, using the leverage to hurl her toward the half-moon window looking out onto the street. The glass and wood splintered outward as she crashed through it. Through the rain of debris, Ashe heard her body hit something four stories below.

He went to the window and looked down. Kali had landed on a wrecked car. She was lying on her broken back, and her eyes looked up at him in shock and disbelief. Ashe slipped through the window and scuttled down the side of the old building, easily finding hand-holds in the bricks and ornamentations.

As he walked toward the car and Kali, the Crow descended from the darkness and landed on his shoulder. Ashe saw that it was watching Kali with its golden eyes.

When he was next to the car, Kali made a moaning sound and struggled to rise, but only her left hand moved, and her head rose a few inches. Her words were a tortured gasp.

"I . . . can't . . . move. . . ."

Ashe merely stared at her. He felt nothing from her, but she might be able to make him feel. Judah Earl's tower waited, but Ashe had to know.

"Kill . . . me, then . . . finish it."

"Tell me something first," he said softly. "Why?"

"Why. . . ? Why what. . . ?"

"Why did you do it? Why did you shoot my son?"

Her face, even filled with pain, was as blank as ever. "Why. . . ?" She took a rattling breath. "Because it *felt* good . . . that's why."

Ashe put his hand on her shoulder, bracing himself for the shock of her pain, all the things that had made her what she was, that had brought evil to her life. But to his amazement, he felt nothing. He sensed no pain at all beyond the physical agony she was now undergoing. Her soul was empty.

He drew back his hand. "You *chose* this," he said, and could not understand.

"Kill me. . . ." she repeated. "Please. You have to."

Ashe shook his head. He looked at her prone body,

saw the predators gathering in the shadows of the alleys. Wherever there was mayhem, they were there to pick up the pieces, get a little for themselves.

"My job is to send you to hell," Ashe said. "You're in it."

Kali stared at him, and at last he saw her eyes go wide with fear. The mien of the stoic warrior had evaporated at last. "There's no . . . *honor* in this. . . . It's my . . . death. And death is . . . all I've ever wanted. Give it to me! *I've won it.*"

"Me too," Ashe said, and turned away from her.

"Wait!" she cried after him. "Where are you going . . . ? Wait! You can't . . . do this! You can't. . . ."

Her words trailed off weakly. Ashe left her in the cold, wet street and walked to the end of the alley where he had left his motorcycle. He heard the laughter and the voices of the wolf-pack gangs as they discovered what had been left for them:

Hey hey, look what we got here. . . .

A kung fu babe, man . . .

Nah, motherfucker, she's a metal mama. . . .

Well, who's got the fuckin' can opener?

Drag her back there. . . .

No, into the car . . .

Not enough room, just yank out the seat. I'm first, man. . . .

How come you first?

I got the gun, motherfucker. But don't worry—she ain't goin' nowhere. . . .

Oh yes, Kali was in hell, sure enough.

The Crow took wing, and lifted its way into the night while Ashe fired up his motorcycle, drowning out the shouting and the whining, tearing away from Sarah's building in a cloud of smoke that could not begin to cover the ugliness of the scene he left behind.

He rode toward the tower, and Judah Earl. And Sarah.

Sarah was dreaming of Ashe Corven. He was at the bottom of a great pit, and the walls were made of water. She was on the other side of the pit, somehow under the ground, and all she had to do was push through the water, and she would be with him.

But every time she touched the wet wall, it broke apart, letting more water rush into the pit, and she would draw back in terror. Her need to be with him would make her try again, and every time it was the same. The more she tried to go to Ashe, the higher the water grew. And as her desperation increased, Ashe came closer to drowning, until at last the water was up to his face.

She pushed one more time, aching to be with him, and finally the water flowed in and covered his head, and she watched him drowning. . . .

Her eyes fluttered open to a thread of drifting smoke. Burning candles surrounded her, and they smelled of alien, bitter incense. She was lying down, her cheek against cold tile. Slowly she uncurled her body and sat up, disoriented, still partly in the dream, not knowing where she was.

She moved her arm and found that it was shackled to something, and then she saw, beyond the candles, great pillars ringing her. The chain was attached to one of these. The metal looked old and rusty, and she yanked at it several times, trying to snap a weak link, but it did not give. Then she looked around, trying to get her bearings. She remembered the warrior woman and the two men breaking in, and fighting them, but everything after that was black.

Overhead she saw a webwork of steel girders. She seemed to be in a large tower, and through decorative openings at the top, she thought she could see the red-orange lights of the city.

Then she looked more carefully at the darkness beyond the pillars, and sucked in her breath when she saw a figure standing just a few yards away, cloaked in darkness, head bowed. It seemed like a ghost, and Sarah sensed that it was waiting for something. For her? Then she would ask it a question.

"Where am I?"

The voice that came back was filled with infinite sadness, even more so than those of Eric and Ashe, who had been to life's other side and returned. "You are in the tower. Everyone finds their way here eventually."

Sarah stood up unsteadily. Her muscles felt cramped and aching. She stretched, getting out the kinks, and then moved toward the woman. Whoever this creature was, she did not seem unkind, and Sarah put a hand on her shoulder, to persuade her to help Sarah if she could, and also just to prove to Sarah that she was real and not a spirit of some kind.

At the touch of Sarah's hand, the woman raised her head with a start, and her hood fell back. Sarah gasped at what she saw. The woman's eye sockets were hollow, with no eyes to fill them out, and the lids had been sewn together with black thread.

"My God," Sarah said in awe of what stood before her. "What happened to you. . . ?"

"Fate happened to her."

Sarah spun around and saw a tall, gaunt man emerging from the shadows between the pillars. His black clothes and funereal manner made him appear to be a part of the darkness out of which he had stepped. "Sibyl has been cursed," the man went on, "with the gift of prophecy. She sees things that are fated to happen."

Sarah looked at the woman again. Before the disfigurement to her eyes, Sibyl might have been pretty, even beautiful. Sarah could not begin to guess her age. She might have been anywhere from twenty-five to a well-preserved fifty.

"She cut her eyes out with a carving knife," the man said, walking to the side of the blind woman, "because she wanted to make the visions stop." He brushed his hand against the back of the seer's cheek, and Sarah saw an affection there that suggested the pair might once have been lovers. "But that only made the visions stronger. Didn't it, dear?"

Sibyl jerked her head away, shunning the caress. "I've learned to live with my affliction," she said.

The man took a deep breath. "Don't we all."

Then Sarah knew who he was. The tower in which she was imprisoned, the decorative ironwork above them, around the top. She backed away, wary but angry as well. "Judah Earl," she said.

He bowed his head slightly. "My reputation precedes me."

"I've seen what your drugs have done to this city."

Judah Earl shrugged cavalierly. "I saw a need, I exploited it. It's all economics, Sarah. Supply and demand."

"Why did you bring me here?" she asked, knowing that he didn't have to answer, that he didn't have to do a damned thing he didn't want to. But he seemed arrogant and proud, and people like that were all too quick to talk and brag.

"I'm glad you asked me that, Sarah, because we went to a lot of trouble to find you. Your friend Noah was most reluctant to advise us of your whereabouts, even with such persuasion as only Kali could muster."

"Noah!" She jerked against her chains, but they held fast. "What the hell did you do to Noah?"

"Me personally? Nothing. But as for Kali . . ."

"Who the hell is Kali?"

"You tell me, my dear. Aren't you versed in such things?"

"The goddess of death," Sarah said.

"Oh, she is that. As I think she proved to your little friend."

"Noah is . . . dead?" She felt a great hollow in the pit of her stomach.

"I'm afraid so. The tool of his trade became his undoing."

"What?" Her voice was shaking. "What do you mean?"

"I *mean* that Kali shoved a tattoo needle through his eye and into his brain. But you may be relieved to

177

know that he died silently, unless you count screaming. He did not betray you. He didn't have to. After all, you're here, aren't you?"

"Why?" she said, her eyes filling with tears for Noah. "What do want with me?"

"Oh, don't underestimate yourself, Sarah. You've got a very important part to play in this little drama of ours." He walked toward her, raising a finger as if for emphasis. Though his manner was elegant, Sarah saw with repugnance that his fingernails were long and yellow and jagged. He stopped directly in front of her, his hungry eyes devouring her, his index finger pointing directly at her face. "You see, I intend to capture the Crow . . ."

The fingernail rested on her forehead for a moment, and then she felt a sharp and sudden pain as he slashed the nail once, twice, down and across, incising a cross into her skin.

". . . and you, my dear, are the birdseed."

He stepped back, and Sarah raised her hand to her head, trembling with pain and horror. Then she took her hand away, looked at her palm, and saw an X there in her own blood. "Why are you doing this?" she said.

"Have you ever read Dante's *Inferno*?" he responded. "It says that the only true path through hell lies at its center. If you want to escape it, you have to do what Dante did—go further in."

Judah lowered himself into a chair, next to which was a thick red candle on a wooden holder. He looked at the flame for a moment, then put his head back, looked up toward the top of the campanile, and closed his eyes.

"When I was a boy," he said calmly, "I was skating

with my mother and father on a frozen lake. It seemed safe. The surface looked as though it would support us. But surfaces do not always tell the truth. The ice was thin in one place. I believe there must have been a spring beneath, but we didn't know that then. If we had, my parents would never have allowed me to skate there. They loved me very much, you see.

"It was a beautiful day. Cold, but the sun was shining brightly on the snow, making it sparkle like diamonds. I was wearing a red jacket, bright red, and snow pants, and red mittens. I liked them because I could feel my fingers all together and warm. My mother and father were skating together, her arm linked through his. At times they would separate, and she would do figures. She was an excellent skater, very graceful on the ice, and she looked quite beautiful that day, her cheeks pink with the cold, her eyes bright. She had on a white, fluffy wool hat, and a sweater with reindeer on it."

Judah Earl interrupted his story long enough to fix his gaze on Sarah. "I remember everything so vividly, you see, because it was the last day of my childhood. Things would never have that beauty and that simplicity again. My innocence ended that day." He closed his eyes and resumed his tale.

"I was not a particularly good skater, although my mother was trying to teach me the basic figures. I was skating backward, showing her that I could do it, and I fell. Had I remained on my feet, I might have merely passed over the fatal spot, but I did not. And when I tried to push myself to my feet, I pushed right through the ice. It fell away from me, and I followed it down, into the water.

179

"The shock was so great that I still can't remember feeling the cold. The water soaked through my clothing instantly, pulling me down, and though I knew how to swim, the gentle current from the spring quickly tugged my body beneath the ice, before I could even lift an arm to save myself. I looked up, and through the ice I could see the blue sky. It seemed close enough to touch, and I knew if I could touch that sky, the ice would not be there, and I would live. Then I saw my mother and father up there in the sky. They were both beating upon the thick glass that separated me from them.

"Then the world grew cold around me. Dark. Before they could break through, my heart stopped beating. And in that moment I died."

Judah Earl opened his eyes, raised his head, and looked at the candle flame. He swept his hand through it and pinched it out of existence. A tiny wisp of smoke trailed up, mingling with shadows. He sat back in his chair again, but now he kept watching Sarah, and she shifted uncomfortably beneath the scrutiny of his gaze.

"A half hour later I awoke on an operating table. They had succeeded in bringing me back. I had returned to the world of flesh and bone—but I brought back knowledge with me." He tapped his temple with his bloody nail. "*Forbidden* knowledge. As Hamlet's father, who also beheld the other side, put it:

'. . . But that I am forbid
To tell the secrets of my prison house,
I could a tale unfold whose lightest word
Would harrow up thy soul, freeze thy young blood,

180

Make thy two eyes, like stars, start from their
  spheres.'

"In other words, Sarah, *scary*."

Judah Earl's lambent eyes glowed like hot coals,
and Sarah could not help but wonder what exactly he
had seen in Death's realm. She fingered the ring on the
chain around her neck, and the ankh next to it.

"I should have stayed dead, Sarah," Judah said.
"I've been living on borrowed time ever since, looking
over my shoulder, listening for the approach of Death's
black wings. Other people say they know that Death
waits for everyone, but they don't really. They can't
know what it's like, so they think about other things.
But I know. And I think about it every waking minute
of every single day. And it comes into my dreams at
night. Death is coming for me, Sarah. I just didn't
know what face it would wear.

"I see now that your friend—Ashe Corven—is the
one I've been waiting for."

"You can't stop him," Sarah said angrily. "You can't
hurt him."

"You're wrong, Sarah." Judah stood up, and there
was a confidence in his rough majesty that told her he
was speaking the truth. "To escape hell, you must seek
its center. And to defeat Death . . . you must trade
places with him. *Become* Death."

There was a sudden hiss, and both Sarah and Judah
looked at Sibyl. Her face was turned toward the east.
"The Crow is coming," she said.

Judah looked back at Sarah and smiled, his lips
pressed tightly together, holding his secrets.

181

18

I REACHED THE PORTAL COMMON SPIRITS FEAR,
AND READ THE WORDS ABOVE IT, DARK YET
  CLEAR,
"LEAVE HOPE BEHIND, ALL YE WHO ENTER HERE."
  —James Thomson, "The City of Dreadful Night"

Ashe was riding through the City of Angels toward Judah Earl's tower by the shortest route possible. When he could, he followed the "Jesus Saves" sign, and when it was hidden by other buildings, he kept moving in its general direction by the widest streets possible.

He came screaming over the top of a hill, when a horse-drawn carriage loaded with people suddenly loomed up in front of him, a man in a devil's mask behind the two horses that pulled it. Ashe had only a second to see that the street behind the carriage had been cordoned off with wooden barricades festooned with flashing lights. A street fiesta for the Day of the Dead.

Ashe swerved, braking hard to avoid ramming the

carriage. His bike slipped out from under him, and he rolled on the cobblestones, smashing into the barricades. The skull-masked occupants of the carriage jumped out to help him, but they were amazed to see that the crash victim was up and on his feet, vaulting the barricades and running into the crowd beyond. He soon vanished, and they climbed back into their carriage, and rode on to the celebration of la Día de los Muertos.

The streets were alive now, and roaring with the sounds of the crowd. Music and singing and laughter and shouts rose from the City of Angels, up amidst its highest building, even into the gloomy top of Judah Earl's tower.

The sounds of merriment followed the Crow as it soared up toward the buzzing "Jesus Saves" sign, and wrapped its claws around the blinking neon. Then it dropped down a few yards and entered the campanile through one of the openings in the iron grillwork, and settled again on one of the girders that crisscrossed the top of the tower.

It looked down through the webbing of girders and saw Sarah far below. She was sitting on the floor in a pool of light, chained to a great pillar.

The Crow leaped from the girder and drifted down on its great wings.

Sarah heard only the faint sounds of celebration that drifted into her prison from above. The Crow's wings made no noise as it glided down, so she didn't know it was there until it landed on the floor near her feet. Its *caw* was loud, as though it were trying to tell her something. But she had something more important to tell it.

"Go . . . please go. . . ." she said quickly, waving her arms.

The Crow tilted its head as if it were trying to understand what she wanted, why she did not desire its help.

She picked up her chain and rattled it against the floor, trying to startle the bird into flying away. *"Go!"* she cried, but it was too late.

With a harsh clatter of pulleys and wires, a steel cage came crashing down onto the floor, trapping the Crow within it. It was large enough to hold a crouching man, and the bars were covered with a tight mesh so that there was no way the bird could squeeze out of its prison.

The Crow cawed angrily, flitting from one side of the cage to the other in a frantic but futile effort to escape, stopping only when Judah Earl emerged from the darkness. He crouched down on the floor, studying the bird, and then he grinned.

"Well, well, well. Look who's come home to roost."

On the streets outside the tower, the massive festival was well under way. The area was mobbed with thousands of people celebrating the arrival of the Day of the Dead. The sacred and the profane gathered together, along with those who just wanted to have a good time, never mind the reason.

The vast majority of the people thronging the streets gave no thought to the religious derivation and implications of the festival. Instead they laughed and screamed and drank, and many snorted Trinity, not suspecting how its absence during the next few weeks would torment them, now that the factory had been destroyed.

But all that would come later. This night, this dark day was for merriment, and they danced under the paper "*bienvenidos*" banners to the music of the bands, punctuated by the exploding strings of firecrackers the children lit. Musicians strolled the streets with their guitars and trumpets and fiddles and accordions, masked mummers cavorted in their garish costumes, some wearing single masks that covered their entire bodies. Above the heads of the crowd, giant papier-mâché skulls bobbed on sticks in a forest of torches and *calavera* placards.

Businesses shot up instantly. Stalls offered marigold and cockscomb blossoms by the tens of thousands. There were black beeswax tapers to light for the dead, dangling toy skeletons, made of silent rubber or clattery plastic, and mountains of *calaveras de azúcar*.

Ashe Corven pushed through the suffocating press of revelers, like some latter-day and monochromatic Red Death through Prospero's swollen court. But in this swirling and ribald company, he seemed to be just one more painted face, and moved nearly invisibly amidst the carnival atmosphere.

He looked up past the torches and the skulls, and saw, a few blocks ahead, the words he sought:

JESUS SAVES.

Judah Earl slid the cage containing the Crow over a solid bottom that he snapped into place. Then he picked up the cage, carried it over to a curtain, and beckoned Sarah to join him. Her chain allowed her to come within a few feet of him as he set down the cage and swept aside the curtain, revealing a large table with a concave surface.

"What's that?" Sarah asked.

"A camera obscura. A very old device, but still highly functional. It shows me things, Sarah. And I believe that you will see things on it too." He grasped a lever beside the table and pulled it, opening the camera's lens.

Moonlight shone down on the camera table, and Judah shifted another lever, adjusting the camera's view. On the table, Sarah saw the night sky, filled with stars. It was as if they were in a spaceship, and she was looking down through a porthole into the void. A churning landscape of clouds, lit eerily by the moon, drifted across the table's surface.

Judah reached behind the table and picked up a bundle wrapped in crimson velvet. He opened it, folding back the cloth to reveal a set of ornately decorated daggers in sheaths sewn fast to the velvet. He ran his fingers over the handles like a pianist playing an exquisite chord and looked at Sarah.

"Do you know what these are called?" he asked her, then answered his own question. "Misericords. Wonderful name, isn't it?" Judah daintily slid one of the tapered blades from its sheath, and ran the glinting edge along his finger.

"This was the principal dagger in the Dark Ages," he said. "One purpose was to penetrate the joints of the armor of an unhorsed adversary. Such a dire threat could cause the vanquished knight to surrender 'at mercy,' but most scholars believe the knife derived its name from the fact that it delivered the death stroke, the *coup de grâce,* to the mortally wounded, and so were considered tools of mercy." He looked at the steel cage holding the trapped Crow. "My, how times change. . . ."

He set the knife back on the cloth, and from behind the table took a heavy leather falconer's glove and pulled it over his left hand. Then he opened the door to the cage.

Sarah pulled madly at her chain, but could not stop Judah Earl as he reached inside. The Crow flapped its wings wildly, desperately trying to slash at Judah with its beak and claws, but the leather protected the man from harm. He gripped the bird around its throat and pulled it out of the cage. Its wings still beat madly, and it looked to Sarah as if Judah were holding a black tornado in his hand.

Then Judah slammed the Crow down into the shallow bowl of the table of the camera obscura.

The crowd had thickened near Judah Earl's tower, and had grown more truculent as well. The children were few and far between, and most of the adults were drunk, grabbing at each other and everyone else who passed.

A drunken, masked woman grasped Ashe and spun him around before he could recover. "C'mon, honey, lez dance, lez dance . . . do that ol' Dance of Death, huh?"

She grabbed him again, but he shoved her aside, fighting his way through the crowd until he looked up and finally saw the letters directly above him: JESUS

SAVES. Far overhead, the black sky shimmered with turbulent yellow thunderheads, lit from below by the revels of the city.

Judah Earl's tower was high and wide and anything but handsome. Years of polluted air had coated the building's facade with a patina of filth. Angels and caryatids graced its surface, but they bore mantles of soot and stoles of grime over their formerly white marble. Gargoyles leered down, hard layers of dust on their fangs and tongues. Decorative granite vines grew black and stagnant.

Ashe's gaze slid down the high tower to the double front doors at street level. A massive iron gate covered them, and even if he had been able to get through it, heavy chains were wrapped around both handles. No one was going in or coming out that way.

He looked back up at the campanile. There were dozens of openings in the scrollwork, and he felt sure that he could slip through one of them. Then he examined the statuary and ornamentation on the facade of the tower—gargoyles, caryatids, statues, ledges wide and narrow, a ladder of stone ascending the face.

He took off his duster, dropping it and the sawed-off on the pavement, and jammed the .45 he had taken from Curve into the small of his back. Then he leaped straight up, grabbed the feet of the lowest statue, and pulled himself skyward, starting the daunting task of scaling the tower.

Up he climbed, clinging to marble vines, flagpoles, gargoyles' mouths, the breasts and shoulders of the caryatids. Several stories up, something exploded in Ashe's face, a cluster of feathers and beaks that startled

189

him, so that he nearly fell. For a long moment he dangled by the tenuous grasp of his fingertips until his searching feet found a toehold. He clung to the building, and watched the flock of pigeons he had disturbed soar through the concrete canyons and disappear.

He continued climbing. On the ledge of the tenth floor, he rested for a moment, searching out the best route. The rattling hiss of an ancient window opening made him turn to his left, and there he saw, leaning from the window and glowering at him, a hulking, blond-haired man.

A window ripped open on the other side, and for a moment Ashe thought that he was looking into a mirror that had erased his own reflection, for it seemed that the same blond man glared at him from the other side. He jerked his head back quickly toward the first, and realized that there were indeed two identical twins.

His first thought was to keep climbing, so he leaped for his next handhold and pulled himself up, thinking to leave them behind. They could do nothing unless they caught him. The only way they could delay him was to pull him off the tower, and that was a delay he couldn't afford, with Sarah in danger. He could probably ascend the face of the tower faster than they could climb the stairs.

But he quickly learned he had underestimated their speed and agility. Though thick with muscle, they scampered out the windows and across the ledge, crawling up after him like bulky monkeys, climbing the vines and statues and grimacing faces as easily as a ladder.

He could shoot them, but .45 shots were loud, and

would alert Judah Earl to the trespasser on his tower, if he didn't already know. Still, Ashe couldn't afford to take the chance. So he climbed on, not looking back, hoping to outdistance them.

He was amazed, just three stories higher, to feel fingers clawing at his ankle. Ashe violently kicked free and pulled himself up as he glanced down. One of the twins was nearly on him, and, even as Ashe watched, grabbed him again by the toe of his boot. What was most shocking was that as the heavy man clutched the boot in a death grip, he threw himself backward, as if to hurl them both off the side of the building.

Ashe dug his fingers into the stone as the weight of the man nearly dragged him off the tower's facade. Any other man would have plunged to his death with his killer, but Ashe still had the strength of the Crow. The man slammed back into the wall, and the impact eased his grip long enough for Ashe to free his foot and pull himself up to the next ledge.

By that time, the man's twin was coming at Ashe from the left and below, and Ashe shot up the facade, forgetting caution, reaching blindly and scrambling for handholds where there were none. Several times he nearly fell, but the gap between the twins and himself continued to widen.

Still, there were at least twenty more stories to go, and Ashe knew his luck would run out eventually. He searched for an answer, and when he drew himself up over a particularly rococo section of stonework, he found it.

A large oval window of thick stained glass was set into the stone face, just beneath a protruding ledge.

Wide enough to be seen and admired from the ground, it was ten feet across and nearly eight feet high. Ashe looked down and saw that his pursuers were scarcely twenty feet directly below him.

Ashe leaped straight up, grabbed the edge of the ledge above, swung outward, stiffened his legs, and brought them crashing through the inch-thick window. As soon as they broke the glass, he snapped his knees straight back, spitting the broken, jagged pieces outward, so that they rained down the side of the building, a razor-sharp, fatal hail.

One of the brothers, concentrating on the wall before him, threw his head back in surprise at the sound of the breaking window. A slab of smoky violet glass came slashing down upon his exposed neck. His severed head fell several seconds before his fingers gave way and his body followed, landing upon a wider ledge below. The head bounced off, soaring across the street and landing on the roof of a shorter building opposite the tower.

The other brother was speared in the back by a long piece of glass that had defined the window's border. He also fell to the wider ledge, where he lay watching the blood pump from his dead brother's neck for several minutes before he joined him in darkness.

Ashe pulled himself up past the window, took a deep breath, and started to climb once more.

"Hang on, Sarah," he whispered as he drew closer to the campanile. "It'll all be over soon. . . ."

19

AND DID YOU NOT LOSE YOUR CROW, WHEN YOU
FELL SPRAWLING ON THE GROUND?
                                    —Aristophanes, *The Birds*

"Easy, little wing," Judah Earl said to the Crow. "It
will all be over soon."

The wind had increased outside, and the night
clouds projected on the camera table—and onto the
Crow—rushed by at an unearthly speed, creating a sur-
real backdrop for the bird's frantically beating wings.
It looked to Sarah like a mockery of the Crow's flight,
and she felt shame and pity for it, wishing that it would
stop, that she could do something . . .

. . . wishing that Ashe would come.

"He is here!" Sarah whipped her head around. She
had almost forgotten about Sibyl, standing in the shadows. The seer's head was lifted up, and her face was
taut with knowledge. *"Ashe* is here. . . ."

The words were electric, full of power and portent,

and while they were the words Sarah had wanted to hear, they frightened her. It seemed as though the time had come for the final battle, and she was not ready for it.

But Judah Earl was. He smiled at Sibyl's news, as if the moment had been long anticipated.

"Ashe is here. . . ." he repeated Sibyl's words. "But not for long."

Judah kept his left hand on the Crow's throat, pinning it to the table, and with his right he picked up the unsheathed misericord, raising it high into the air.

"Nooo . . ." Sarah moaned, turning her head away. But she could not turn away from the sickening sound as Judah Earl plunged the weapon down, pounding it straight through the Crow's right wing into the wood beneath.

Ashe Corven was crouching on a narrow cornice, thinking about his next move upward, when white-hot pain lanced through his right hand.

He screamed in agony and clutched his wounded hand with the other, losing his balance and nearly toppling off the face of the building. But he caught himself with effort, gasping at the pain. Then he looked down at his hand, and saw blood seeping from a wound on his palm.

Stigmata, he thought, the wounds of Christ, and his mind whirled. What was happening? He had not been able to bleed before—his flesh had closed up almost as quickly as it was pierced. And now he was bleeding from a wound in his hand? What had happened to him?

Then he thought suddenly, What had happened to the Crow?

Sarah looked back at the camera table. The Crow was pinioned by one wing and Judah Earl's hand was on its throat. The torn wing was bent unnaturally, the feathers fluttering weakly and piteously. Bones were broken, nerves were severed, and she sobbed at the sight.

Then Judah picked up another misericord. He glanced at Sarah and smiled. "Can't have a proper crucifixion with only one spike, can we now?"

He raised it and drove it down. Sarah made herself watch, and her hatred for Judah Earl, already strong, doubled in intensity as the dagger sank into the Crow's left wing.

Ashe, she thought. Come. Please come.

Ashe Corven's left hand was wrenched backward, and fire burned through his palm as if a hot iron had been thrust against it. The pain poleaxed him, and he fell forward, slipping off the cornice and tumbling to the next ledge down, a decorative one as wide as any on the building. He struck on his hip and rolled off, but caught the lip of the ledge with his clutching fingertips.

The pain in his hands made him cry out, but he hung on. For a second he looked down and saw, far below, the crowd celebrating the Day of the Dead. They seemed so far away that if he fell, he thought he would fall forever, and he clung to the ledge, looking up at the backs of his hands.

They both had the mark of the stigmata, and Ashe

could see shards of white bone protruding through the wound in the back of his left hand, as though some invisible being had driven something through it with great force. It took every ounce of strength he had to keep from simply letting go.

He tightened his grip on the ledge above, and the pain in his hands increased tenfold. But he could not let go. He could not.

". . . oh God . . . help me . . ."

My God, why hast thou forsaken me . . . ?

". . . oh God . . ."

He gritted his teeth and pulled with his hands and arms until he began to rise. Then he pressed his feet against the side of the building and slowly worked his way up. His right hand grasped the foot of a statue set above the ledge, and he hauled himself painfully upward, arms and legs trembling, hands and fingers burning, until he had wrapped his arms around the back of the stone maiden, clinging to her like a lover.

He looked into the statue's face. Time and the seasons had worn it smooth, and the acids in the City of Angel's air and rain had eaten most of the details away. The blind stone eyes looked into his own, and in the curve of its cheek, in the shape of its face, he saw:

"Sarah . . ."

For a moment he felt safe. But the moment passed, and he knew that neither he nor Sarah was safe, that they were both close to death. And whatever death might mean for him, it must not come for Sarah.

"Sarah . . ." He whispered the name like a mantra. He had to keep going for Sarah, no matter how great the pain or the urge to give up. The thought of her urged him on, brought strength back to his weary limbs, dulled the burning agony in his hands.

He began to climb without thinking, automatically. It was a job to be done, and when it was, he would do what he had to do. Now only one thought remained: climb. For Sarah.

The campanile seemed as far above him as the sky, which was starting to churn and roil. There was a promise brewing in it of a storm of epic proportions. The image registered in Ashe Corven's dull mind, and he let himself think, Good. Wash it away. Wash the whole city away. Cleanse it. Drown it.

Wash it away.

"The coup de grâce . . . the mercy stroke . . . the end of suffering . . ." Judah Earl picked up a third misericord and held its gleaming blade out in front of his eyes, turning it to catch the light. "The spear in the side."

He raised it high above his head and whispered,

"Ashes, ashes, we all . . . fall . . . *down*."

The dagger fell, and Sarah screamed, and —

—Ashe's cry flew into the night like the soul of a great black bird.

Ripped from his perch by the gaping wound in his chest, he fell, thinking that he seemed to fall faster than his blood, which streamed upward from his heart as he floated away from the sky, toward the ground, just the way he had floated down through the water while his blood remained above, a red cloud mingling with the sea. . . .

• • •

Below on the street, the mob celebrating the Day of the Dead danced beneath the shadow of the unholy ziggurat of Judah's tower. God and the Dead had been forgotten in the hazy river of alcohol and narcotics, and the crowd had been brought to a frenzy by the chemicals in their blood and the music in their ears. Loudspeakers blared, bands pushed their strings and drumheads to near breaking, and the sharp tones of trumpets pierced the listeners' brains like the sound of some stoned last judgment, where God and all the angels were as ripped as the demons.

Louis Thibodaux was having a great time. Five days a week, eight hours a day, he loaded and unloaded the ships that come in and out of the City of Angels. Then on weekends, he worked two six-hour shifts as a short order cook at Alcée's Diner. He hadn't gone inside a church since he was a kid, mainly because he was too busy making enough money to keep him and his wife and three kids alive.

But tonight he had forgotten Marie and the kids and the jobs, and remembered the church just long enough to tell himself that it was the Day of the Dead, and it had *something* to do with church, though he was damned if he could remember what. Ah hell, he told his friend Amedé, he was probably damned anyway, so what the hell.

He knew he had to work the docks tomorrow bright and early at seven o'clock, but tonight was for celebrating. So he sang and danced and drank and told the Trinity peddlers to go to hell when they waved their little envelopes in front of his face. Marie was at home with the kids, and maybe if he met a wild woman, he would . . . well, maybe he would and maybe he wouldn't. It depended on how drunk he got.

And he was pretty damn drunk, but not more than he could handle. He would get wrecked every Saturday night, go home, and fall into bed, and Marie would take off his shoes and put a blanket over him. She was a good woman, Marie. She knew how hard he worked, and she didn't mind if he spent a couple dollars on beer once a week.

Nah, he decided, thinking about Marie, if he met a wild woman he'd maybe give her a kiss, but that was all. He wouldn't use getting drunk as an excuse, even if he *was* a little more wrecked than usual.

Louis looked up to see if the sky above was as wrecked as he was, and he saw Ashe Corven's body falling from Judah's tower.

"Whoa, shit," he said, and nudged Amedé, who looked up too. Hundreds of bulldozed faces followed suit, and they saw the dark angel, arms spread like wings, fall out of heaven down into hell.

The man came crashing down atop a small vending stall filled to the brim with flowers and sugar skulls. The impact threw thousands of marigold petals skyward, and splintered pieces of sugar skull swirled outward twenty yards from the stand. Louis threw up his arms to protect himself from the sweet shrapnel, but it bounced right off of everything it hit.

As the petals fluttered back to the earth, it seemed to Louis that time had stopped. The musicians had fallen silent, the crowd had stopped its singing and shouting, and everyone's eyes were on the crushed stand, and the man who lay atop it.

"Maybe," Louis said to Amedé, "we oughta see if that guy's okay. . . ."

The Crow was dead. The shallow wooden bowl that was the focus of Judah Earl's camera obscura was filling up with its blood.

Two of the gleaming misericords pinioned its wings, and the third pierced its heart. Under the image of the night sky thrown upon the table, the blood that ran from the bird's body appeared as black as its feathers.

Sarah blinked tears from her eyes and looked at Judah Earl. He had stepped back from the table, an expression of horror on his face, as though he was overwhelmed by what he had done, the enormity of his crime.

But the expression faded, and was replaced by a grim look of determination. "It's done," he said in a low voice.

The blood continued to run from the Crow's body, pooling underneath it, more blood than Sarah thought such a small body could hold. It kept flowing, filling the bowl of the table to the brim, nearly covering the dead body of the Crow itself. The Crow's beak and the long flight feathers of its wings protruded from the pool, as did the misericords. They looked like tall grave markers in a field of slaughter.

"Look," Judah Earl said. "Do you *see*?" Sarah moved closer to the table so that she could see the surface from above. The blood had turned the camera obscura into an eerie reflecting pool, and the clouds that rushed across the table were now red. As Sarah watched, the wet surface seemed to ripple from the force of the winds high above, blurring the image, and when the trembling blood stilled again, the only image she saw was Judah Earl's shimmering reflection.

She could not come near enough to stop him as he dipped the fingers of his shaking right hand into the pool of blood like a worshiper into a font of holy water. He brought his index finger down across his right eye, dipped it into the pool, and made the same motion across the left. Then he moistened his fingers again and ran his bloody hand across his lips, leaving a wide, red smear.

Sarah realized with horror that it was an emulation of the ritual in which she had painted Ashe's sorrowful face, but there had been something sacred about her act and Ashe's acceptance of it. What Judah Earl was doing was an obscene parody of their ritual, like reading the Lord's Prayer backward, or celebrating a black mass with a baby's blood.

Only now the blood was the Crow's, and on Judah's face Ashe's mask of irony had become one of cruelty and sadism, demanding acquiescence and inspiring only terror.

"Do you understand, Sarah?" said Judah, his unholy glee making his face look even more frightening. "What Sibyl said—'The life force that flows within it.' Isn't that right, Sibyl?" The blind woman stood in the shadows, but said nothing. "The life force," Judah repeated dreamily. "The blood of the Crow . . ."

Judah Earl put his hands, palms down, into the bowl of blood, then cupped them together and raised them

201

again, lifting several ounces of the blood to his lips. He drank, putting his head back as the blood of the Crow ran down his throat and trickled over his chin and neck. Sarah saw his thin throat working as he swallowed ... swallowed ... swallowed. Then he licked his palms and lifted his head to the heavens, waiting.

It didn't take long. His eyes rolled back in his head so that only the whites showed, and he threw back his arms as if to welcome what had come upon him. It was, Sarah thought, the state of a shaman, possessed by spiritual ecstasy.

Judah Earl's pallid features began to glow with a kind of beatific radiance, as if the blood he drank had gone into his cheeks. But there was more to it than that. His entire frame seemed electrified by something outside himself, something strong and mighty and demanding, something no one could deny or refuse, a force that would claim everyone some dreaded day.

The power of Death itself had flowed into Judah Earl, and he laughed at the glory of it, laughed in Death's face, laughed because he had *become* Death, and no longer had to fear it.

"The guy is *dead*, man," said Amedé to Louis. "What you mean, see if he's okay?"

Louis shrugged and belched. The beer tasted better going down than coming up. "I mean maybe the stand, you know, she broke his fall or something."

"You see how far he fell? *Sacre!* He dead fo' sho'."

Louis wanted to check anyway. There was something about the guy's descent that really had reminded him of an angel come flying down. Only this one flew

could will himself to fly into the night sky with
. The sheer number of the birds fascinated and
ened him at once.

tore his gaze away from them long enough to
at the faces in the crowd of people that sur-
ded him. They were nearly all masked, and the
s of those who were not had been masked by drugs
liquor. They were all still, however, frozen as if in
middle of a dream. Their eyes staring through the
ks were still part of reality, but Ashe seemed on the
ed edge of that reality, unsure if time was working
ot.

hen something beside the crows and himself
ed in the crowd. A child wearing red-and-black
ey and the same type of skull mask that adorned
any of the others walked to the front of the crowd
nd Ashe. The eyes looked at him through the holes
e mask, and Ashe sensed something familiar about
a. But no, that could not be. . . .

en the child lifted the mask from his face, and
saw that he had been right. "Danny . . . ?" he
joy filling his heart. His limbs felt light once
n, his body and hands were healed and whole, and
aped from his deathbed of crushed flowers and
ed to his son's side.

put his arms around the boy and wept with de-
and love. It could not be, and yet it was. Danny
here with him, alive and warm. Their arms were
nd each other. The last thing that Ashe could recall
falling off the tower. Was he dead then? Truly
? And did that mean he could return with Danny?
Oh God . . ." Ashe said, wiping the tears from his

down real fast. And the way the marigold petals had just made a cloud when the guy hit—well, hell, there was something almost magical about it.

And even if he *was* dead, Louis just wanted to see what the guy looked like. So he set his skull mask up on top of his head, since the damn thing had been making his face sweat anyway, and joined the people who were gathering around the crushed stand. Louis pushed his way through the ones who were too scared to get closer, and then he saw the guy. If he was dead, he sure looked happy about it. He was lying on his back, his arms at his sides. The impact of his fall had made a little crater in the array of marigolds and sugar skulls, so that it looked like he was lying in a coffin filled with flowers. Not a bad way to go, Louis thought.

The guy's face was painted pretty weird, like that harlequin in the picture Marie had hung on their bedroom wall. Only the harlequin was dressed in black and white, and this guy just wore black. The whole thing looked like the funeral of a fallen angel, and Louis wondered if, instead of some drugged-up asshole who had fallen off a tower he was trying to climb, this guy was Lucifer.

Hell, even if he'd been sober, it might have made sense. The guy *looked* like some dark angel, and the way he had fallen was weird, like he was lying in state, when he should have been splattered over half the city. Besides all that, it was still quiet, like everybody knew something major had happened. Nobody was singing or yelling or playing music. It was just like thousands of breaths were all drawn, waiting for something to —

Then he heard it, high up in the air. It was like a million people whispering all at once, or wind roaring through the cypress trees in the swamps, or . . .

Wings.

Louis looked up. They all did, a thousand skulls staring into the night sky above Judah's tower. But where storm clouds had raced, where traces of lightning had flickered, where the moon had struggled to shine, all was hidden from sight by the crows.

There were thousands of them, their black wings filling the heavens, blanketing the sky, and now they began to wail, and the high-pitched keening made the hair on Louis's neck stand on end, and set his teeth on edge. They swirled about madly, as in the grip of a storm, an endless army of carrion creatures, shrieking in anger.

What the hell did they want? Louis wondered. Who had they come for?

AMI, ENTENDS-TU
LE VOL NOIR—DES CORBEAUX—SUR
    PLAINES . . . ?
(FRIEND, DO YOU HEAR
THE BLACK FLIGHT—OF THE CROWS—
    PLAINS . . . ?)
                            —"Song of the

Ashe Corven's eyes opened, and the few watching him instead of the crows over and shrank back.

He didn't see them. Part of him was stil bosom of bliss. The last thing he wanted waken from a dark place where there was a loud and garish nightmare of skull face ing sinners.

But he had heard the cries of the crows, remain in sleep's arms no longer. When cused, they focused on the murder of great murder indeed, he thought sleepily remembered everything, and knew that dream.

He sat up, staring at the crows, his b

own eyes with unpierced hands. "God, Danny, Danny, my boy . . . what are you doing here?" He drew back from the boy, holding his shoulders and looking at him, just letting his eyes drink in the sweet sight of him.

"It's time to go back, Dad," he said in the voice Ashe had never thought to hear again. Danny was smiling, but just a little. He looked up at the crows.

Ashe followed their gaze. "Is that why they're here?" he asked his son.

Danny nodded, and looked back at Ashe. "They're the souls who came before you, the ones the Crow brought back to do what they had to do. They're on the other side now. But they came back because of you. They're crying for the people they lost." He put a hand on his father's arm. "Dad, now they're crying for you."

Ashe continued to look at the screaming crows in the sky. He wondered if Eric Draven's spirit was among them, come to call him back to where he should be. But would Eric want him to desert Sarah?

He turned back to Danny. "But Sarah still needs me."

The boy shook his head. "You don't understand, Dad. You work for the dead, not the living. And your work here is done."

Ashe felt as though he were being ripped in half. Here was his son with him at last, and beyond them was the peace he had sought, the peace he had killed for.

But above them in the tower was Sarah, in danger of her life, held captive by a madman who spent lives like pennies. He could not leave her there. In spite of the

207

brief time that he had known her, he knew that he loved her, perhaps as much as he had ever loved Danny.

"Danny, I'm sorry," he said, and his words tasted as bitter as bile. "I can't go, not yet, not now. . . ."

"You *have* to, Dad!" It was more than the plea of a small boy. There was strength in it, and a wisdom that Ashe did not possess. Still, he could not relent. Danny's spirit was free. Sarah's was not.

"Danny, I can't leave her like this. . . ."

The screaming of the crows increased in volume, and when Ashe looked up, it seemed they had grown in number as well. He saw only an ever-moving, shifting mass blotting out the sky, stars, moon, and all.

When he looked back at Danny, a shadow was passing over his face, a sadness far beyond the knowledge of a child. When Danny spoke again, it seemed that another voice spoke with him. Something else had taken command, something wiser and far older than Danny, an entity that was not used to being disobeyed.

"If you turn your back on the dead now, you'll be trapped between the worlds. You'll *never* be allowed to cross over."

Then Danny spoke alone, and his words broke Ashe's heart. "I'll never see you again, Dad. You'll be alone. Forever."

Forever. Ashe hesitated for a moment, already feeling caught between two worlds. If he remained to help Sarah, would he remain always, living without death? Would he age and ache and molder with cancer but be unable to die? Would he ultimately yearn for death like a lover, or with the agony of the addict for the drug he

208

needs desperately and can never have? A bed in some forgotten corner of a hospital, and whispers of a poor, sick man who can never die—was that to be his fate?

Then he thought of Sarah, and what she needed, and his decision was made.

"I have to stay," he said so softly that he wasn't sure Danny would hear.

But the boy heard, and nodded. "I know." He put out a small hand and touched his father's painted face. When he said, "Good-bye, Dad," there was so much loss in his young voice that Ashe nearly changed his mind. But he couldn't. He had chosen.

"Good-bye," Danny said again, and the sounds of the world came rushing back into Ashe's ears. People were talking in drunken confusion, and above, thunder rumbled over the flapping wings of the murder of crows.

Danny started to turn away, back into the crowd, but Ashe wanted to explain, and called after him, "Danny, wait. . . ."

He reached after his son's disappearing form, but instead, found himself reaching up to the sky.

It was empty, save for the rushing clouds and the sickly moon and the haze of filth the City of Angels had thrown into it. He was lying in a bed of crushed sugar and flowers, and his hands and chest ached viciously.

A man with a skull mask on the top of his head stared at him, mouth agape, then smiled, and called to someone back in the crowd, "Hey, Amedé! He dead fo' sho', my *ass*!" Then the man looked back at Ashe and laughed as if he were crazy.

What had happened? Ashe wondered frantically. Had he been dreaming? He looked at the place where Danny had reentered the crowd, and thought he saw the boy slipping into the midst of the throng. Ashe pulled himself off of the crushed marigold petals and ran in his direction, scattering the onlookers standing amazed at his resurrection.

Yes, it was Danny. He wore the same red and black motley, but now he had pulled the skull mask back down over his face again. He ran swiftly amid the press of adults, and Ashe pushed through them, trying to catch up. But the boy scuttled around the people like an eel around rocks, and Ashe despaired of catching him.

Then he saw the short, masked figure slow down near a scantily dressed woman, as though intending to talk to her. The pause gave Ashe time to reach him, and he called Danny's name, touched his shoulder, and spun him around. He knelt and pushed the mask up, not wanting to explain himself to still another face of death.

But instead of Danny's smooth young face, Ashe found under the mask the leering, grimacing, gap-toothed grin of a drunken dwarf. "Danny . . ." Ashe said feebly.

"Sure, pal," said the dwarf. "Shit, I'll be Danny or Franny or whoever the fuck ya want, ya gimme another bottle," and he grabbed his crotch and started to laugh at the horrified expression on Ashe's face.

Ashe recoiled, bumping into several people as he backed away. They spat stoned curses at him as the dwarf continued to cackle at him. Thick, yellow mucus hung from his flattened nose, and strings of saliva dripped from his gaping mouth. The laughter smelled like stale beer and rotten teeth.

Ashe continued to back away, and was pushed to and fro by the celebrants he bumped into. He turned and ran then, ran back toward Judah Earl's tower. At last it stood before him, and he went running toward its locked doors, his hands burning with pain, his chest aching and hollow, and his heart weeping.

Suddenly the doors burst open, shattering the iron gates, ripping apart the chain through the handles as though it were ribbon.

Judah Earl stood before him at last.

21

. . . THE KNAVISH CROWS
FLY O'ER THEM, ALL IMPATIENT FOR THEIR HOUR.
—Shakespeare, *Henry V*

"Ashe Corven," said Judah. "I'd know you *anywhere*."

The face glared at Ashe through the surface of a mask. Ashe saw at once that it was intended to be similar to his own, only it seemed to be painted in red. Or in blood. But with Judah's eyes glowing like twin stars, and his lips curled back into a feral snarl, it seemed like nothing so much as the face of an Antichrist.

No, Ashe corrected himself. An Anti*crow*.

Judah Earl proudly looked behind him at the door he had just blasted open. Ashe thought that it must have been explosives that had smashed apart the gate and burst the chain, but why would Judah have done such a thing to his own tower? He looked deliriously happy at whatever turn of events had breached his fortress. Or maybe he was just insane.

He looked at Ashe again, and Ashe tensed, preparing to spring and make this man pay for what he had had done to Danny, and had done to Sarah. But before he could move, Judah Earl was in front of him, grabbing the front of his shirt and dragging him close, so that Ashe breathed in Judah's breath. It was strong and ripe, as though something had crawled into the man and died, and it made Ashe Corven dizzy.

Looking into Judah's face was almost like looking into a mirror. Ashe saw himself, only twisted, perverted. Two sides of the same coin.

"Tell me, Ashe," Judah husked out. "Do you ever get the feeling we're all just dead men on leave?"

Hatred for the man who held him surged through Ashe. *"Judah,"* he spat out.

"In the flesh . . ." It was only a small movement. Judah drew Ashe another inch toward him, and then flung his arms out a foot from his body. But the move threw Ashe back several yards, and the revelers scattered as he plowed into them.

This was the end, Ashe thought. It stopped here. He reached into the small of his back and pulled out the .45 pistol that he had taken from the body of the dying Curve. It had nearly a full clip, and he jacked the slide, slamming a shell into the chamber.

Then he pointed it straight at Judah Earl and pulled the trigger—once, twice, three times—aiming right at the crime lord's chest.

Judah Earl just stood there grinning. He didn't even stagger. The bullets had made holes in his chest, for

Ashe could see the wisps of smoke rising up from where they had burned the fabric of Judah's clothing, but he did not fall.

Ashe had never felt so terribly disoriented, not even when he had first burst from the sea during his resurrection. Judah Earl was not like him, not a dead man come back to life. What had happened?

"What . . . are . . . you?" he asked, staring at the man in awe.

Judah reached down and picked up a length of the chain that had been blown off the door handles. "I'm your shadow, Ashe. Every angel's got a devil. Didn't you know that?" He examined the chain while he talked, tugging at every link. They all held. Then he looked back at Ashe. "Or maybe you just slept your way through Sunday school?"

Judah Earl lashed out with the chain, swinging its bulky weight as easily as if it had been a piece of clothesline. Its heavy end wrapped around Ashe's chest, slamming into it like a giant mailed fist. He spun away from it, faltered, and fell, shocked and astonished to find himself feeling the pain. The stigmata and the wound in his chest had been mysterious enough, but now he seemed like any other mortal.

Why? Had he turned his back on heaven and been damned as a result?

Louis shook his head, took his mask off all the way, and let it drop to the ground. Hell with it, it was only two bucks, and the damn strap was cutting into his chin. Besides, he didn't want it slipping down over his eyes during *this* show.

215

He had been happy as hell when the weird guy came to. He had even teased Amedé and started laughing, the way he'd always thought Jesus would've done when he brought that Lazarus back to life. Hey, it was a *happy* thing, right? Living, that is. And there was something that he liked about this guy. His face was painted all weird, but Louis thought he seemed *right* somehow.

But then the guy starts acting weird, chasing some zonked-out dwarf, and then the door of Judah Earl's tower smashes open, and Judah Earl comes out, and they start doing these macho bits on each other. And finally the black-clothed guy pulls out a piece and blasts Earl with it.

Louis nearly shit himself, and both he and Amedé hit the deck and got ready to run like rabbits. But Judah Earl just stood there with holes in his clothing where blood ought to be pouring out. Then Louis finally figured it out.

It was a show. Maybe Judah Earl was a drug-selling son-of-a-bitch, but he was getting into the spirit of things by hiring this stunt guy to fall off his tower into that stand, and then blowing open his front door and doing a face-off with him, complete with blanks or a bulletproof vest or whatever the hell they used.

A rich guy entertaining the little people. Louis had heard enough about Judah Earl to know that he was slime, but if he was putting on a free Wild West show, hell, Louis would watch. And these guys were *good*.

Everybody was digging on it, stoned, straight, or otherwise, and the crowd whooped and gasped as Judah Earl swung that big chain out and walloped the

216

guy with it. Then Earl started pounding on the stunt-man, one shot after another, pushing him back with each one. It looked like Earl was really slamming into the guy's face and gut, and they must have rehearsed it pretty good to make it look so real. But shit, if this guy could fall thirty stories or so and live, Louis figured he could slip a few punches without harm.

Whoo, that was a *good* one there. The stunt guy spun around, and fell down on his hands and knees. When he looked up, Louis could see what looked like blood on his lip, and the guy shook his head like he was clearing it. "One of them blood pellets like they use in the movies, huh?" he said to Amedé, who nodded knowingly. They and their wives went to the movies together once a month, and they watched a lot of videos on the VCR, so Louis knew how this stuff worked.

But before the guy could get on his feet, Judah Earl came over and kicked him in the face. Louis flinched and hissed in a breath at that one. The kick flipped the guy over on his back, but he jumped up right away, so Louis knew the kick couldn't have been real.

"Man, that was good, don't it?" Amedé said. Louis chuckled at the phrase. The more excited Amedé got, the more he sounded like his swamp-living *frères*.

Now it was the stunt guy's turn. He ran at Judah Earl, brought his fist back, and threw a real sweet hook at the drug kingpin's face. But Earl caught the fist in his left hand and squeezed. Louis saw Earl's fingers tense like wires, and heard what sounded like the bones in the stunt guy's fist breaking with a series of sharp cracks.

217

"So how'd they do *that* one?" Amedé asked.

"Got me," said Louis, shaking his head.

Ashe Corven's right hand felt like so much crushed pulp, but the pain seemed inconsequential when Judah Earl's fist caught him in the left temple. Ashe spun around and collapsed on the cobblestones.

He tried to push himself up again, but his right hand crumbled beneath him and he fell back on his side. He coughed, spitting up bright blood from his cut mouth and black blood from hurts deeper down and farther in. Then he crawled forward, trying to get away from his tormentor, his dark nemesis.

But suddenly Judah Earl was in front of him again, sneering down at him, holding the heavy chain. "What . . ." Ashe said, sharp barbs stinging his throat with every word, "What did you . . . *do* to me . . . ?"

"I've taken your power, dead man," Judah said. "I've tasted the blood of the Crow, and taken all your power."

Ashe staggered to his feet, telling himself that it couldn't be true, that Judah was a liar and the father of lies. But before he could take a single step forward, Judah's arms became a blinding blur, and Ashe heard the chain whirl and sing in the air. Then something bit into his neck, and he could not breathe.

He could feel his eyes bulge as he toppled again to the street, the chain wrapped around his neck. The fingers of his left hand clawed at it, and his shattered right hand fumbled, but to no avail. Judah Earl pulled him forward, choking, and crouched over him like a spider ready to devour its prey.

"In case you hadn't noticed, Ashe, you're flesh and blood now. You can suffer and die like any other man."

Suffer? Yes, Ashe thought. But die? That he wasn't so sure of. But he only answered Judah with three words that crept in agony from his throat: "Go to hell. . . ."

Judah didn't lose his smile. "Already been there," he said. "And I must confess, I liked what I saw."

"Heavy shit," Amedé said, and Louis had to agree.

"Yeah, but it's the Day of the Dead . . . so I guess Earl's gonna pretend to kill the guy."

"Can you hear what they're saying, though?"

"Nah." Louis could see the actors' mouths moving, but he couldn't hear a thing over the excited murmur of the mob. "Hell, they go to all this trouble, they oughta have mikes, am I right?"

"Fo' sho'," Amedé said, watching the show. "I mean, how you supposed to follow the story?"

"The *plot*," Louis corrected.

"Ah yeah. The *plot*."

Sarah sobbed quietly, still chained to the pillar in Judah Earl's campanile. Everything was lost. The Crow was dead, and Judah Earl had its power. The last Sarah had seen of him, he had vanished, laughing insanely, into the shadows, and she had heard nothing more. Even the sounds of the celebration in the streets below had quieted, and she wondered what grim tableau was taking place down there.

From the little she had seen of him, she knew that

Judah Earl was not one to hide his powers. He would use them, and she feared he would use them on Ashe.

Sibyl had said he was there, and she prayed that he would not be harmed, prayed that he would come for her and end this, end Judah Earl and his madness, before he . . .

She didn't know *what* he could do with his new powers, but she was sure he would not use them for good. An invincible man with the power Judah already had could rule the city. He could terrorize and kill, let the people know what he was capable of, and what he wanted.

There might even be some who would think him a god, or God's deputy on earth. He could dethrone the pope, gather armies . . . the possibilities were limitless and terrifying. Judah Earl was Death walking abroad.

But how could she stop him? What could she do if Ashe was weakened, if the powers the Crow had given him had died along with the Crow itself?

What would she do if Ashe was dead?

The thought put the taste of metal in her mouth, and she shook her head. It could not be. As terrible as it was to imagine a world in which Judah Earl ruled, it was worse for her to think of a world without Ashe.

She loved him. She could admit it to herself now. At last she knew what Eric had felt for Shelly, because it was what she felt for Ashe. She would have died for him, but she hoped to be able to live for him. But chained as she was, she could do nothing, and her tears were bitter and angry.

"Sarah . . ."

For a mad second she thought it was Ashe, but when

she looked up she saw the shrouded form of Sibyl standing next to her. Perhaps she had a key. If Sarah leaped to her feet and overpowered her . . .

But the thought died stillborn as, from the folds of her robe, Sibyl drew out a key and slipped it into the lock of Sarah's manacles. She turned it, and the chains fell away like magic. Sarah was free.

It couldn't be this easy, she thought. Was it a trap? Sarah looked at the blind oracle, uncertain what to do next. "Why?" she asked Sibyl. "Why are you doing this?"

Sibyl's face centered on Sarah, and she had the unpleasant sensation of not only being seen by a blind woman, but being *known* completely. "Ashe needs you now. More than ever."

She folded back the long sleeve that covered her other hand, and Sarah saw that she was holding one of the misericords, the daggers of mercy. She extended it handle first.

"Go to him," she told Sarah, and gestured into the shadows beyond the pillars.

Sarah grasped the handle of the knife and raced in the direction Sibyl had pointed. She ran through a beckoning, dimly lit doorway, past a grime-smeared placard with the printed words THIS IS NOT AN EXIT, and down a short hall that ended at an open elevator door. The conveyance was old and rickety, but Sarah dashed inside, pulled the accordion-fold security gate shut, and punched the down button on the tarnished brass control panel.

The elevator lurched, then began to move with a

wheeze of rusty gears and cables, starting its slow journey downward.

Come on! Sarah thought. Hurry . . . please hurry!

Alone in the campanile, except for the *scratch . . . scratch . . . scratch* of the captive stag beetle, Sibyl listened to the rattle of the elevator, and wished Sarah Godspeed. It was time for Judah to die, and though she could not have killed him, she could turn loose those who could, let slip the dogs of war to raise the havoc she could not.

She had loved him once, the same kind of unselfish love that she knew Sarah felt for Ashe. She supposed she still loved him, or the thought of what he might have been. But he could never stop looking for Death over his shoulder.

Even when they had made love, he had never truly been there. He was always listening, watching for something in the night. When she received her gift and her curse, and tried to drive the visions from her eyes with sharp blades, she had become ugly to him. Ugly but useful. He had sewn her eyelids together himself, so that he would not have to look into the empty sockets, and had sung to her as he worked.

And then she watched too, watched for Death moving through the world, drawing near to the tower. At last it had come, and he had become it.

Sibyl thought of the line from John Donne—"Death, thou shalt die"—and hoped it would be so. She tried to see what would happen, but could not.

It could go either way, then. This future was balanced on a razor edge, and it would take little to throw it to one side or the other. She hoped that her freeing of Sarah would help tip the odds in the favor of life. Sibyl had had quite enough of Death.

She crossed to the table where the Crow lay pinioned, and removed the three misericords. She hurled them into the darkness, ashamed of her crime, filled with guilt that she had helped to do this thing. Her empty eyes would have wept if they could.

Then she dipped a finger into the pool of blood. The liquid felt cool and clean, like the water of baptism. Cleanse me, she thought. Forgive me. End this now.

22

O Lord! You can even see the crows flying. Lord have mercy on us sinners!

—Leo Tolstoy, *War and Peace*

Judah's foot was planted on Ashe's chest. He pulled on the chain with both hands, tightening it around his victim's neck even more. Ashe made a thin, choking noise in his crushed throat.

"Do you see your precious Crow, Ashe? Do you see his blood on my face? Do you hear it moving through my veins? It looks like your avatar's gone. The dead have forsaken you, my friend."

Ashe's fingers, broken and whole, tapped feebly at the chain, and Judah's lip curled in a mocking snarl.

"Look at you, bleeding like a stuck pig. Where's your precious strength now? Where's your power?" Judah chuckled, and struck a fist against his own chest. "It's *here,* greater than ever." He leaned down and whispered in Ashe's face, "You're nothing now, Ashe. Not even a *ghost*."

Judah Earl straightened up, grasped the chain in both hands, and started to walk backward down the street, dragging Ashe behind him. Ashe whimpered in pain as the rough surface of the street sawed through his clothes, rubbing his body raw in a hundred places.

On the east side of the street, several storefronts ahead, was an abandoned movie theater. In the early sixties, Louis's grandfather had taken him there several times to see shows. Louis was so young that he had no idea what was going on up on the big screen, but he had thought that the theater itself was a wonderful place.

There was a huge lobby inside, and paintings on the ceilings and a gigantic Oriental rug on the floor. Inside, the theater was like some Moorish palace, with arches and pillars and a bas-relief bridge over the forty-foot-wide screen. Louis always liked sitting in the balcony so that he could see as much as possible of the theater's opulence.

That glory extended to the outside of the theater as well, and even now, twenty years after the theater had closed for good, the marquee stood proudly overhead. Though the neon letters were long dark, the twists and curves spelling PARADISE looked as though they could shine anew at any moment.

The memories flooded through the half-drunk Louis as he and Amedé followed the crowd up the street toward the theater. Judah Earl and his sidekick were putting on one hell of a show, one that Louis would never forget. For a second he wished that Marie were there to see it, but then changed his mind. It was much too violent for her.

Now Earl was next to the Paradise marquee. He stopped walking, but kept holding the chain in one hand. Using his other hand, he pulled himself to the top of a stall selling crawfish, and from there he clambered to the top of the marquee, twenty-five feet above the mob.

His eyes looked like they were on fire, and Louis wondered if he had some special kind of lenses or something. Then he shouted to the crowds, his voice so loud that he didn't need a mike.

"You want Death? Here he is, people! Take a good look!"

On the ground, the stunt guy had managed to get to his feet, and looked like he was trying to get the chain from around his neck. But Judah Earl wasn't going to let that happen. There was a street lamp whose pole stuck straight out from the side of the Paradise Theater, and Earl looped the end of the chain over it, held on, and jumped down to the ground.

As Judah Earl descended, the stuntman went up, yanked off the ground by Earl's weight. His hands still tore at the chain around his neck, and his dangling legs started to kick.

"These guys got really strong neck muscles," Louis observed to his friend.

"Nah," said Amedé. "My grandpère told me 'bout a show he seen in Paree—they did *everything* there—cut off people's hands, burned out their eyes, branded 'em, hung 'em, and it was all phony. They had these fake necks went around their real ones, Grandpère said. . . ."

Louis nodded sagely. All fake. Still, he was glad it wasn't him dangling up there like some poor bird caught in a snare. The guy's shirt had been nearly torn to shreds. Probably wearing some flesh-colored mesh vest underneath. He shook his head in respect. These guys were *professionals*.

At last Ashe knew the curse that his remaining on earth had brought him. He could suffer like any other man, but still he could not die.

The chain crushed his vertebrae, keeping the air from his lungs, the blood from his brain, but still he would not die. He could be tortured for days, months, years of endless agony and pain, and he would not die. He knew that this was all the hell that anyone could fear.

He felt himself swinging from Judah Earl's noose, but there was no way down. The chain was too tight around his throat to loosen. His bulging eyes showed him Judah Earl hauling down harder on the chain, lifting Ashe higher into the air, impossibly tightening the noose even more.

Then Judah wrapped the end of the chain around a fire hydrant and secured it there. He walked, as casually as a man out for a Sunday stroll, to where Ashe was hanging, and circled him, looking him up and down, inspecting his work, grinning like the cat who swallowed the Crow.

"Now don't we look pretty," he said while Ashe struggled, choked, kicked, legs jerking in the air, a marionette operated by an epileptic puppeteer. "How are you feeling, Ashe? Sorry now you took my loyal, clean-cut helpers away from me? All choked up about it?" He laughed. "That was terrible, I know. But you have to laugh anyway. You always have to laugh when God cracks a joke. If you don't, you suffer the punishment."

Suddenly something fluttered away from Ashe's thrashing form. It swept through the air like a large butterfly and landed at Judah Earl's feet. It was Danny's tattered painting that Ashe had kept with him, and had now fallen from his pocket.

Judah knelt, picked it up, and unfolded it. It was stained in a dozen places with Ashe's blood. Judah turned it this way and that, appraising it from all angles. Finally he gave his verdict.

"Nice craftsmanship . . . shows a fine mastery of form, but I particularly appreciate the primary medium." He looked up at Ashe, his eyes full of crazed humor. "If you prick him, does he not bleed?"

Then, very deliberately, his gaze fixed on the struggling Ashe, he tore the painting into shreds, letting the night wind blow the pieces away, sending them up into the air, scattering them toward the dark clouds above.

"So much for the permanence of art," Judah said, chuckling at the white-and-red pieces of paper being swallowed by the updraft. "Now let's try a little experiment concerning the permanence of *pain*."

Next to the theater was a partly demolished building. Beneath a scaffolding, jagged pipes and rusty iron supporting rods protruded from crushed concrete like pins from a giant's pincushion, and Judah strode over to them. Grasping one of the rods, he wrenched at it, breaking off a four-foot length as easily as if it had been a dead branch.

Then he returned to where Ashe was hanging, stripped the last few shreds of clothing from his bloody back, and stepped back, holding up the rod. "And now, Mr. Christian," he said in a round, pompous voice, "ten thousand of the best, if you please . . ."

He brought back his arm and whipped the iron rod directly at Ashe's back. The rusty metal tore into his flesh with bone-breaking impact, and white-hot fire shot through every nerve in his body. His eyes rolled up, and his body screamed at his brain to surrender, to die, to fall into the blackness of shock and unconsciousness, but he could not.

He could only absorb the beating, blow after blow after blow, of the monster who was hell-bent on thrashing him into oblivion.

"Stop him!" Sarah cried, trying to push her way through the crowd. She had entered a scene out of hell. The swirling faces of the masked and bare-faced celebrants were an always moving wall between her and Ashe. The crowd was in the grip of a mob mentality. Everyone seemed to be drunk and laughing at the dangling fool and the harsh disciplinarian before them, a warped Punch and Judy show for the aged children of the City of Angels.

"Stop him!" she screamed again, pushing against a man in a devil mask.

He turned toward her and pushed back. "Christ, honey," he said, "it's just a fuckin' *show*. . . ." Even through his mask, she could smell the reek of cheap wine on his breath.

"It's not a show!" she shouted at him. "It's *real*!"

His response was a shrug and a laugh. "So what?" he said. "It's still balls-out entertainment, ain't it?"

His laughter followed her as she maneuvered around him, and the sound was swallowed up by the other laughter and shouts. She had to make them see that it was real, had to tell them what was happening.

But if they knew, she thought with a thrill of horror, what would they do? What could they do to Judah Earl?

She pushed and pushed, making headway, catching glimpses of the main attraction, Judah and Ashe, between the bobbing heads of the roaring mob. Oh God, poor Ashe . . . the skin of his back was hanging in strips, and what looked like a soaking red sponge oozed beneath. Then the rod came down again.

Sarah gave a cry of rage, and leaped over the last few people who kept her from Ashe, body-surfing over their surprised heads and shoulders as their legs buckled from the contact. She rolled onto the street, only a few yards from Judah Earl.

"Get away from him!" she cried, lunging forward, the misericord in her clenched fist. Judah turned, startled, and Sarah drove the long, tapered blade directly into his right eye.

He staggered back, clapping his hand to his face, momentarily blinded. Sarah dashed to the chain around the hydrant and, after a few seconds of effort, freed it. The chain clattered over the lamp pole as Ashe fell to the street.

Sarah watched him, afraid to move, afraid that he was dead, but hope filled her as she saw him sit up and loosen the chain at his neck. It fell onto the ground, and she was about to run to him when he looked at her and shouted.

"Sarah, look *out*!"

She swung around, but it was too late. Judah Earl was rushing toward her, one eye dripping blood and fluid. She started to throw up her hands, but Judah drove the misericord roughly into her chest. She could hear her breastbone crack, and felt hot ice enter and claim her.

Sarah dropped to her knees, clutching at the dagger's handle. She felt her fingers wrap around it, her muscles contract, felt it slide from her body with the ease and limpness of a spent lover. It dropped to the street in front of her, and she put her hands over the wound it had made. Blood trickled from between her fingers, over her hand, and into her lap. She looked at her red hands as though she could not believe what she saw, and then fell back.

In the sudden silence, Louis felt Amedé's hand on his shoulder. "Louis," his friend whispered in hushed awe, "I don't think this a show."

"I think you dam' right," Louis whispered back to his friend, reverting to the patois of his youth in his alarm. He was suddenly afraid for the man and the woman, and very, very afraid for himself, for what he had seen and done nothing to stop. "This real, fo' sho' . . ."

Ashe sensed the whole crowd beginning to move backward as a mass, as if what they had come to laugh at and cheer for had unexpectedly become something very different. He dropped to Sarah's side and put his hand on her breast, trying to stop the flow of blood, but it was no use. She looked at him, and then up past him, toward the sky, and her eyes widened in wonder.

"The crows . . . I can see them coming. . . ."

Above, wheeling around the ceiling of the sky, were the thousands of crows Ashe had seen when Danny had come back for him. But Ashe didn't see them now.

He saw only the woman he loved, her life bleeding away, and Judah Earl, the man who had taken that life, and so much more.

Reason fled Ashe Corven's mind. All that was left was unbridled animal fury, the righteous rage that had never stopped burning since his resurrection. Only now it was stronger. Now there was even greater loss.

Ashe launched himself at Judah Earl, who couldn't have begun to expect such a forceful attack from a man who had just been hung and beaten. Judah went crashing back into the nest of scaffolding next to the theater, struck with such power that the jagged end of one of the pipes punched right through his chest, impaling him.

The crowd gasped, and Judah Earl screamed in shock and surprise as he hung there, pinned like a butterfly on a board. But then he started to laugh, and Ashe knew it was because he felt no pain. Judah grasped the pipe that sprang from his heart, and began to pull himself along it toward the end, cackling hysterically.

"You can't stop me anymore, Ashe!" he cried. "You don't have the power! You don't—"

But then Judah stopped, seeing something in Ashe Corven's face. A beaten man didn't look like that. A beaten man fell down and died, and his eyes didn't keep boiling with hatred.

"If it were just me," Ashe said, "you'd be right, Judah. But I have an *eternity* of pain to call upon . . ."

Ashe looked at Sarah, and lifted up his hands, exposing his bleeding palms.

". . . and the pain gives me *strength*!"

Ashe raised his painted face to the thousands of crows twisting and turning in the night wind, his brothers and sisters in agony, those whose pain had been so great that they could not die until they had eased it with the balm of justice.

He *felt* their pain, the pain of a man whose eleven-year-old daughter had been beaten and raped before his eyes by three men who then killed them both . . .

. . . the pain of a mother whose divorced husband stabbed both of their children to death, and then cut her to ribbons . . .

. . . the pain of a father whose entire family was blown to pieces by a bomb planted by fools who thought innocent blood could transform the world to their own vision . . .

. . . the pain of Eric Draven, its strength recalled, to feed the soul that needed strength.

And the balm of their pain, of so many thousands so near, healed Ashe's wounds. The stigmata closed themselves up like eyes shutting fast, the blood drawing itself back into the torn palms. He could feel the exposed muscles in his back grow new sheets of flesh, and the bones of his neck and ribs and hands knitted themselves together, grew whole and solid and strong.

Then Ashe Corven raised his voice and his spirit to the heavens, to the circle of pain, the cloud of black birds. Alone, Ashe could do nothing to Judah Earl that Judah could not survive.

But Ashe was not alone, and he cried out for help: *"Take him!"*

And they descended.

A murder of crows.

It spiraled down from the sky like a black tidal wave, a dark cloud of death. Ashe saw Judah Earl's eyes grow wide with terror, and then he was blotted from sight as claws and beaks fell upon him like a storm of razor blades, a single entity whose only goal was destruction.

Judah's shriek rode high and far over the flapping of the crows' wings. Then it stopped as the muscles that made it were plucked apart and ripped away. Blood ran from under the blanket of crows, rivulets of it, trailing serpentlike into the street and around the feet of those who watched in horror, unable or unwilling to move, fearful that they might be next. Pieces of cloth and pale flesh flew into the air like grain from a threshing machine, and the wet, sucking sound of flesh leaving flesh continued for a long time.

After the first few seconds Ashe saw none of it. He turned away, returning to Sarah's side.

"Ashe . . ." she said weakly, raising her arms as best she could. ". . . hold me. . . ."

He knelt and picked her up effortlessly. If only he could have given her his strength . . . even his life. "You can't die, Sarah," he said, thinking that the mask of irony the gods wore must be smiling now. "Can't you see—*I stayed for you!*"

Her breathing was becoming more and more labored, but she was able to speak. "There's a balance . . . that needs to be kept. Someone had to . . . cross over." She winced as a wave of pain washed over her, then took a ragged, bubbling breath. Ashe saw blood on her lips. "I didn't want it to be you. . . ."

Her effort to smile filled his eyes with tears, and he blinked them away, wanting to see her alive for as long as he could. Ashe felt her blood wetting his arms, and thought how pale her face looked. Her life was fading away before his eyes. He saw his own tears dropping on her breast. The drops were tinged with stars of black and white, the paint of his mask washed away by his sorrow.

Then in a voice choking with anguish, he told her the saddest thing he knew, the saddest story he had ever heard. "I can't go with you, Sarah. I have to stay here now." He broke down in tears, and her beautiful face faded in his eyes. Every word came like the thrust of a knife in his own heart. "I . . . have . . . to . . . *stay*."

He felt her fingertips brushing away the tears from under his eyes. "Do you love me?" she said in a whisper.

He could not speak. His throat was closed with sobs.

So he nodded, and hoped she could still see, that the light had not yet dimmed in her eyes.

Her hand left his face, and Ashe was afraid that it had fallen onto her breast, and that she was dead. But when he rubbed away his tears, he saw that she was holding the ring on the chain around her neck. Her knuckles whitened, and with great effort, she snapped the chain apart. She slid the ring from it, and held it up to Ashe.

"Take . . . this."

He took the ring, and she closed his hand around it. Her fingers were so cold. He kissed them to warm them.

"I'll wait for you," she said. "*Forever*, if I have to . . ."

Forever.

She shut her eyes, and rode out another wave of pain.

"Oh God . . ." Ashe said, praying, cursing, begging.

"Listen . . ." The word was scarcely a breath, and he put his ear down to her mouth. ". . . if two people . . . really love each other . . ." She inhaled sharply, clinging to breath, to her life, just long enough to tell him what he needed to know.

". . . nothing can keep them apart."

Her last word floated away on her dying breath.

"Nothing . . ."

Ashe nodded. He would keep the thought, wear it as close to his heart as he would wear the ring. They were the only two things he had left to cling to.

Sarah's eyes lost their focus. Her head went slack in Ashe's arms. Her spirit had fled.

Ashe lowered his lips to hers, kissing her for the first

and the last time. Then he cradled her lifeless body in his arms, rocking gently back and forth, and let the tears stream down his cheeks.

He heard what sounded like a distant fluttering of wings, and when he looked up, the crows were gone, and so was the body of Judah Earl. All that remained was a crimson puddle, and a single crow perching on the pipe on which Judah had been impaled.

The bird looked at him, but he could read nothing in its golden eyes, and in another second it too flew away, up into the night.

In the empty glass poster displays of the Paradise Theater, Ashe saw himself holding Sarah, the hollow-eyed, masked celebrants all around them, as if waiting for something more to happen, and Ashe knew he had seen the image before.

I paint what I see.

It was the picture Sarah had been working on, the woman dying in the arms of her lover, surrounded by the silent dead. The picture was finished, the last strokes in place. It was time for everyone who had a home to go to it, to fold their covers around them like shrouds, to drift into the arms of Sleep, Death's kind brother, and be thankful they were still alive on this Day of the Dead.

Ashe started to walk, Sarah in his arms, and the crowd slowly parted for him, revealing a golden path of marigold petals leading down the street. No one spoke, except one man who had his arm on the shoulder of his friend. Neither was wearing a mask.

"I'm sorry," the man said to Ashe, and there were tears in his eyes.

Ashe gave no answer in word or gesture. He walked on. It was not his to forgive what had happened this night.

The crowd parted before him, and closed behind him as he passed, holding Sarah in his arms.

"Oh my God, Louis," said Amedé, shaking his head. "It was all real. We maybe coulda stopped it, maybe coulda kept that *fille* alive."

"We was all here, Amedé," Louis said, wiping his eyes with a big red handkerchief. "And we none of us did nothing."

"Does that mean we all bad, Louis?" Amedé sounded frightened of that possibility.

"I don' know, Amedé. I don' know. But maybe we all try to be better, eh?" Louis looked around at the crowd quietly dispersing. "This suppos' to be the City of Angels, and it's filled with the ghosts and the devils." He watched the man walking away, holding the dead woman, far down the street. "I don't know 'bout them. Maybe they the angels."

Amedé gave a little snort. "The way they do, with the knife and the birds? If they angels, Louis, they dark ones."

"She jes' tryin' to keep her man alive, and he gettin' back at the one what killed her. Hell, any angels better than none at all. C'mon, let's get to home. It been one hell of a night."

They walked in the opposite direction from the one the dark angels had taken. Louis looked up at Judah Earl's tower, and wondered what had started all of this in the first place. All he knew was that it was a place he never wanted to go. Home was good enough for him.

At the top of Judah's tower, Sibyl stood over the table of the camera obscura. The Crow was gone. Not a trace of blood remained.

Sibyl saw the street below without eyes, and knew what had happened there. She nodded to herself, satisfied. Judah was dead, or at least the total entity that had been Judah Earl.

If one could have looked closely at the small, nearly microscopic bits that the crows had rent apart, if one could have peered with the eye of knowledge into the red stain that was all that remained of Judah Earl's physical countenance, one might have seen a motion beyond the cellular level, a twitching of those tiny, tiny pieces that would never stop, not even after hoses washed them down the storm drains, and they drifted into the Styx and floated out to sea.

They were Judah Earl, the immortal one. They would never die. And they would never stop knowing the pain of their separation from one another. Judah Earl was, and always would be, an infinity of agonies.

The trace of a smile crossed Sibyl's lips at the thought, and she closed the curtain for the final time over the camera obscura. The campanile, the tower itself, would be left to fall into decay, a tomb for Judah Earl's evil. There was only one more thing she had to do.

Sibyl walked slowly to the table where the stag beetle was tethered to its nail. From within her robe, she took a small pair of scissors and cut the thread that bound it. Free at last, flung out of its constant orbit, the beetle scurried out into the universe, over the edge of the box, across the table, down onto the floor. It disappeared into the shadows.

Sibyl gathered her robes about her, and followed suit. The darkness welcomed the one who knew it so well.

Dawn came hard to the City of Angels. The sun's rays touched the highest towers almost reluctantly, and then, when they were not renounced, gathered courage and went on, pushing the shadows down the sides of the buildings, into the deep canyons of the city, where shadows always lived.

It was there that Ashe Corven walked with the burden of the woman he loved, dead in his arms. He had not known where to go, and finally arrived by chance where chance had taken him the night before, to the small church where he had seen the *offrenda* and learned about the Day of the Dead before he had had to live it.

He entered the sanctuary, and after all the effort of the night before, Sarah's body seemed no heavier than when he had first picked her up. Her death had rendered her frame as light as air in his arms, but he knew he could not bear even that ethereal weight much longer. There was another, more demanding weight he had to carry forever in his soul.

The church was still aglow with candles, even more so than when he had visited it before. But it seemed empty. No worshipers sat or knelt in the pews, no grieving mothers or fathers or wives or husbands or lovers made offerings at the altar.

No matter. Ashe had the sweetest offering of all.

He walked down the center aisle to the front of the sanctuary. There he stopped and lay Sarah's body down in front of the *offrenda*. He folded her arms across her chest, and rolled a shirt, an unused gift for the dead, into a pillow and placed it under her head so that she looked as though she were sleeping.

He touched her cold hands for the last time, and rose. Then he stood looking down at her, letting his eyes drink in her beauty, knowing that he would never see her again, in this life or the next.

But he thought about what she had said, how she would wait for him forever, and how nothing could ever keep them apart. "Forever," he said softly, and turned and walked up the aisle.

As he was passing through the nave, the old priest he had met the night before came out of the narthex, and looked surprised to see him. "You're still here, my son? Why?"

Why *was* he here? Why in this world and not the other? Ashe told him the truth. "Because I have nowhere else to go."

He stepped past the priest and moved toward the daylight beyond, wondering how he would live in it. "What will you do, then?" asked the priest.

Ashe looked back at him. "The city is filled with shadows. One more won't make it any darker."

He walked out onto the street, blinking at the sun, surprised by the strength of day. After being in the dark church, the light hurt his eyes, and he found shelter for a minute in an inset doorway, huddling in its shadows.

Finally he opened his hand. He had kept it clenched into a fist from the moment Sarah had given him the ring that had belonged to Shelly, another woman lost before her time. He turned it over in his hands, reading the word, FOREVER, etched on the inside. He closed his eyes and held the ring against him, inscribing the word on his soul. Then he slipped the ring onto the ring finger of his left hand. He had thought it would be too small, but it was not. It fit perfectly, and there it would stay.

"Are you all right?"

The voice came as a surprise, especially its tone of concern, and he looked up quickly. A girl stood a few feet away. She looked about fifteen, and her skin was healthy and glowing, her golden hair falling free and clean around her shoulders. She was carrying a cat in her arms, and after a closer look, Ashe realized that she was holding Gabriel.

"Long night, huh?" the girl said, and the cat meowed as if in agreement. Ashe nodded, then reached out and rubbed behind Gabriel's ears. The cat closed its eyes and purred with pleasure. "Isn't he cool?" the girl said. "I found him on the street. Guess he doesn't have a home, so I thought maybe I'd take him home with me."

"You should," Ashe said. "Looks like he needs a home."

The girl grinned and hugged the cat. It purred louder. "Well, see ya," she said, and turned around to walk away.

There was a small purple bag hanging over her shoulder, and a big yellow beaded happy face was sewn on the side.

"Hey!" Ashe called, and the girl turned around. "What's your name?"

The girl cocked her head, as if wondering why he wanted to know, then shrugged and told him. "Grace. My name's Grace. How about you?"

"Ashe."

"See ya, Ashe," she called gaily, and started back down the street. Gabriel turned around in the girl's arms and looked back at Ashe over her shoulder.

Ashe moved out of the shadows of the doorway into the steadily growing light, watching Grace and Gabriel. Grace. The little Trinity junkie.

Maybe Sarah could perform miracles after all. Here was one.

Ashe hoped for another.

24

THE CITY IS OF NIGHT, BUT NOT OF SLEEP;
  THERE SWEET SLEEP IS NOT FOR THE WEARY
     BRAIN;
THE PITILESS HOURS LIKE YEARS AND AGES CREEP,
  A NIGHT SEEMS TERMLESS HELL.
        —James Thomson, "The City of Dreadful Night"

I believe there's a place where the restless souls wander. Burdened by the weight of their own sadness, they cannot enter heaven.

And so they wait, trapped between our world and the next, endlessly searching for a way to rid themselves of their pain—in the hopes that somehow, someday, they will be reunited with the ones they love.

I believe it's true, for I have seen it happen.

Ashe closed Sarah's journal. He sat back on the couch in the loft, watching the lights of the city through the open half-moon window. She was here.

She was here in the shattered mask, the slashed canvases, the bent and twisted furniture and the clothing strewn all about. Here in the shards of broken mirrors, in the shadows of broken dreams.

She was here in her final painting, and so was he, and so was Death.

And she was here in the book he held in his hands. Her thoughts, her visions.

Her hope.

Hope was all that Ashe had now, and he slipped the small journal into a pocket against his heart. Then he looked around the ruined loft for the last time and set a burning match to the great pile of Sarah's things he had gathered in the middle of the floor.

By the time he reached the window, the entire loft was ablaze, and as he climbed down the front of the building, the flames cast his shadow, as dark as the wings of a great Crow, onto the street.

His motorcycle howled its power to the night, and he opened the throttle and began to ride.

There is a land. . . .

There is a land the living cannot know, where the mist hangs like tears, a thick cloud of pain and sorrow as impenetrable as it is endless.

Through that primordial realm of shadow a bird flies. It is a crow, its feathers black as night, and behind it blindly gallops a steed with unending strength. Mounted upon it is the rider whose eyes look out from behind a painted mask, where black accents at eyes and mouth highlight white flesh.

It is a mask of irony—laughter and despair and pain and love and sorrow are all intermingled in its simple lines, its upturned smile, its hash-marked eyes that drip dark tears.

The black-lined mouth moves, and a single word falls from it like a rock into a pond, heavy as lead, yet buoyed with hope—

Ashe . . .

And the woman rides on, dreaming of another land far away, and a man she loved there. She rides, always grieving, always hoping, searching for the bridge, the tunnel, the valley or hill over which she will ride that will bring her to—

Ashe.

There is a land of the living . . .

. . . and through it rides a dead man who cannot know Death again.

He came back to this land seeking the justice that would bring him rest from his pain. He found it, but he also found love, and, again, loss.

He rides a mount of steel, as tireless and powerful as the warrior's horse, and he wears the selfsame mask of irony as the woman's upon his doomed and haunted face. He races through the night, sweeps through the forest of the city, rides the shadows, looking for some way into the land where the woman he loves has gone, the woman whose name falls from his black-rimmed lips over and over—

Sarah . . .

They are worlds apart.

They are traveling the same road.

For though in reality these lands are far from each

other, in truth they are one and the same. And truth is wiser and kinder and more merciful than reality.

And so they ride apart but together, separate but one, and hope that someday truth and reality will blend the way their two souls have blended, each to the other, despite the distance of different worlds.

They are one.

They will be one again.

If two people really love each other, nothing can keep them apart.

Nothing.